TREASURE HUNTERS

PERIL AT THE TOP OF THE WORLD

BY JAMES PATTERSON
AND CHRIS GRABENSTEIN

ILLUSTRATED BY
JULIANA NEUFELD

FOLLOW THOSE BEAR TRACKS!

1 3 5 7 9 10 8 6 4 2

Young Arrow
20 Vauxhall Bridge Road
London SW1V 2SA

Young Arrow is part of the Penguin Random House group
of companies whose addresses can be found at
global.penguinrandomhouse.com.

Penguin
Random House
UK

Copyright © James Patterson 2016
Illustrations by Juliana Neufeld

First published by Young Arrow in 2016

www.penguin.co.uk

A CIP catalogue record for this book is available
from the British Library

ISBN 9781784754310

Printed and bound by Clays Ltd, St Ives Plc

Penguin Random House is committed to a sustainable future
for our business, our readers and our planet. This book is made
from Forest Stewardship Council® certified paper.

MIX
Paper from
responsible sources
FSC
www.fsc.org   FSC® C016897

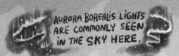

AURORA BOREALIS LIGHTS ARE COMMONLY SEEN IN THE SKY HERE.

THE NORTH POLE ★

SOME SNOWDRIFTS LOOK PINK BECAUSE OF FERMENTED BIRD POOP. EW!

GREENLAND

NORTH AMERICA

THE UNITED STATES

★ NEW YORK CITY

#6 WHERE BICK AND I HAD TWIN TIRADE #329. THAT ONE WAS A DOOZY.

MEXICO

MAYAN PYRAMIDS

CENTRAL AMERICA

ATLANTIC OCEAN

PACIFIC OCEAN

SOUTH AMERICA

CHILE

★ SANTIAGO

CHILE'S NATIONAL SPORT IS RODEO.

TREASURE?

THE **WORLD** ACCORDING

ARCTIC
OCEAN

Tip: WOLVES REALLY LIKE SPICY MEATBALLS, AS WE FOUND OUT.

HELSINKI

MURMANSK

RUSSIA

ST. PETERSBURG

MOSCOW

BUTYRKA PRISON
WHERE WE WERE SENT TO PRISON! NOT. SO. FUN.

ASIA

EUROPE

ITALY

FLORENCE
NEARLY 1/3 OF THE WORLD'S ART TREASURES LIVE IN FLORENCE.
MOLTO BENE!

PACIFIC
OCEAN

AFRICA

YOU'LL NEVER GUESS WHAT TABLE MOUNTAIN WAS NAMED AFTER!

UH, ACTUALLY, IT'S NOT THAT HARD TO FIGURE OUT...

INDIAN
OCEAN

CAPE TOWN

AUSTRALIA

SOUTHERN
OCEAN

To THE KIDDS

NEW ZEALAND

WATCH OUT FOR HOBBITS!

N W E S

ANTARCTICA

QUICK NOTE FROM BICK KIDD

Before we launch our latest heart-stopping, nail-biting, globe-trotting Kidd family adventure, I just wanted to let you know that, even though our parents are both back in the picture, I'll still be the one telling you our awesome tales. My twin sister, Beck, will still be handling the pictures (including the ones that Mom and Dad are back in).

And get this— Mom and Dad have promised to take us around the world again before we grow up: Asia, Europe, Africa, Australia, the Americas, North Pole,

ASSORTED EVILDOERS

South Pole, and all the points in between. Trust me, you'll remember going around the world with the Kidds for the rest of your life.

Beck says I should add, "Especially if you stand downwind of me." (Apparently, I reek in ways that are amazingly unforgettable.)

Now, can we get going? We're kind of in a hurry. Don't forget—we have a whole world to circle!

PART 1

THE TREASURE HOARDERS

CHAPTER 1

There are all sorts of art treasures in Florence, Italy—including the stolen kind.

That's why the six of us—the entire Kidd family—were crammed into an electric, solar-powered van staking out a garage on a dark cobblestoned street in the middle of the night.

The street was so old and narrow, it was probably built way back in the Middle Ages before the rich Medici family jump-started the Renaissance by sponsoring guys like Michelangelo, Raphael, Donatello, and Leonardo (the artists, not the Teenage Mutant Ninja Turtles).

Mom was behind the wheel. Storm was up front, keeping her night-vision goggles trained on the garage entrance. Dad and our teenage brother, Tommy, were in the back, where you're supposed to stow luggage. They were both decked out in commando gear: black shoes, black pants, black turtlenecks, and black watch caps (Tommy complained his was giving him a serious case of hat hair).

Beck and I were in the middle seats. As the youngest, we were supposed to "sit still and observe" because this mission could, according to Dad, "go south fast."

"You guys?" I whispered as Mom and Storm focused on the parking-garage entrance. "This van is powered by solar panels. How's that going to work at night?"

"Batteries," said Storm.

"Something you might want to try for your brain," added Beck.

"Twins?" said Dad from the way back. "Can the chatter, please. We don't want to compromise our position."

That's spy lingo for *Don't get us busted with your loud yapping.* Dad and Mom used to work for the CIA, helping to keep America safe. Now we're on an even more important mission: saving the world's treasures—and I don't mean just ancient art and artifacts (or, in Tommy's case, this "awesome hair gel" he discovered in France).

Sometimes I think Dad and Mom want us to save the whole entire planet!

5

CHAPTER 2

We were in Italy staking out this particular parking structure because Mom had picked up a hot tip from the pirates who had kidnapped her in Cyprus.

The bad guys kept yakking about smugglers transporting an elaborately decorated 2,600-year-old mummy sarcophagus through Florence.

And it wasn't empty. There weren't any wrapped-up pharaoh remains in the ancient coffin, but Mom's captors said all sorts of precious pottery and sculptures were hidden inside. The "importers" would be handing it off to the "exporters" in this garage.

"EM 429TY," said Storm from her perch in the passenger seat. "It's them."

Storm has a photographic memory, so she's in charge of memorizing stuff like bad guys' license-plate numbers. Mom and Dad's spy friends (the kind of friends with satellites) had been tracking the smugglers' cargo truck as it made its way into Florence from the Mediterranean seaport of Livorno.

"They're pulling into the garage," said Mom as she flipped down her night-vision goggles. It's still weird seeing her with blond hair. She had to dye it so the bad guys wouldn't recognize her. Spy stuff. "Their arrival was expected. Two men just came out of the shadows."

"Let's roll," Dad said to Tommy. "Bick? Beck? Mic check."

Beck and I tapped our chests to activate our supercool tactical headsets.

"Testing, one, two, three…"

"Loud and clear," reported Mom.

"Tommy and I are going in," said Dad. "Bick and Beck?"

7

"Yes, sir?" we said at the same time.

"You two follow us and report back to Mom and Storm. However, you are not, I repeat *not*, under any circumstances, to enter that garage."

"No, sir."

"You mean 'Yes, sir'?"

"Yes, sir."

"Good. Okay, Tommy. Charge up."

Dad and Tommy slid battery packs into their Taser weapons. They didn't want to shoot any bad guys with bullets, but they'd stun-gun them if they had to.

Mom turned around in her seat.

"Thomas?" said Mom. "Be careful in there."

Of course, she was talking to both of them: seventeen-year-old Tailspin Tommy and Dr. Thomas Kidd (aka Dad).

But she meant my father particularly, and for good reason.

We'd just found out Dad was alive. We didn't want to lose him again.

8

CHAPTER 3

Beck and I followed Tommy and Dad out of the van and crouched behind a row of Vespa motor scooters.

We couldn't really see what was going on inside the garage.

So we crept closer and found a hiding spot beside a pair of rusty trash barrels.

Uh-oh.

Things didn't look so good. In fact, things looked *molto, molto male*, which is Italian for "very, very bad"!

Tommy and Dad had their hands up over their heads.

"You two *idioti* don't know who you are dealing with," growled a muscular goon who looked like he might be a former member of the Italian weight-lifting team. "The ones we work for are *appassionati d'arte*. Very serious art lovers. You do not wish to make them your enemies."

"Of course we don't," said Dad. "Our only wish is that you—and those you work for—return that stolen mummy to its rightful owners: the government and people of Egypt."

"Chya," added Tommy.

"We do not have time for your noble speeches," said the guy who was apparently the head goon, waggling a pistol. "Turn around. Massimo? Handcuff them both. *Sbrigati!*"

"*Sì, sì, sì,*" said the muscleman named Massimo. He quickly chained Tommy and Dad to a pole in the center of the garage.

Why do bad guys always have chains lying around?

I tapped the chest switch to my mic. "Mom?" I whispered. "The bad guys are handcuffing Dad and Tommy!"

"What should we do?" asked Beck.

"Stay put," said Mom. "I'm calling for backup."

"But—"

"Stay put! The *polizia* and the *carabinieri* military force will block the front door with vehicles. They'll apprehend the suspects when they try to roll out of the garage."

We watched two of the bad guys take the mummy case out of the first van and load it into the back of an antique cargo truck with *Vesuvio Olio di Oliva* painted on the sides of its canvas flaps.

"Careful!" cried Dad. "That sarcophagus is nearly three thousand years old!"

The bad guys ignored him.

"Aprite l'uscita segreta," the lead goon barked to two of his henchmen. Then he grinned at Dad and Tommy. "We have a secret rear exit." He tapped a stubby finger on his caveman-like forehead. "Smart, no?"

Uh-oh. That meant they'd anticipated our plan.

One of the bodybuilders thumped a big green button on a box attached to a thick electrical cable. A section of what looked like a brick wall at the far end of the garage rolled up. It was a metal garage door painted to look exactly like bricks.

They have some very good mural artists in Florence.

13

"Let's go," I said to Beck, forgetting that my mic was still open.

"Bickford?" said Mom. "What do you think you're doing?"

"Keeping this whole mission from heading south!" I said, trying my best to sound like Dad.

While the bad guys fiddled with their secret door, Beck and I crouched and then made a dash for the tailgate of the truck where the canvas flap in the back wasn't tied down.

We hoisted ourselves up and over the tailgate and hid alongside the thousands-year-old coffin.

The engine started up. Gears clattered. With a lurch and a bump, the truck moved out of the parking garage through the secret exit. With us hidden inside!

Where were they taking us?

CHAPTER 4

"**B**ick? Beck?"

Mom's voice was urgent in our ears.

"Rebecca? *Bickford?*"

Yep. She was also mad. That's just about the only time she ever calls us by our full names.

"Where are you two?"

I looked at Beck. She looked at me. The truck hit a pothole or maybe bounced off a curb.

"You tell her," whispered Beck. "You're the wordsmith."

"We're, uh, um…in a truck. An olive-oil truck. With the mummy."

"What?"

"The bad guys drove through the back wall of the garage and—"

"Bickford Kidd, you—"

After some whispered yelling that you don't really need to hear about, Mom told me what I should do. I raised the side flap and peeked out at the street.

"We're on the Via Palazzuolo," I said, reading a sign.

"The *polizia* and *carabinieri* have arrived," said Mom. "They've already apprehended the two gentlemen who dropped off the sarcophagus."

"What about Tommy and Dad?" I asked.

"They're fine," said Mom. "You should be seeing them shortly."

"Huh?"

"Do you have your phone?" asked Storm over my headset.

"Yeah."

"Make sure the GPS is on."

"It is."

"We'll track you," said Mom. "So will Dad and Tommy. Hang on, Stephanie!"

17

That's Storm's real name. And Mom's the only one who can call her that without her eyes turning into dark, threatening thunderclouds, which is the reason we call her Storm.

The truck took a sharp left turn. The mummy slid sideways toward Beck and me. We stopped it with the soles of our tennis shoes so it wouldn't get knocked around and even more damaged.

Bouncing along, I smelled water. "We're near the river," I reported. "I think."

"Roger that," said Mom. "We have you on the Lungarno Amerigo Vespucci."

Then, of course, Storm jumped in with one of her travelogue monologues. "The long boulevard along the Arno River is named after the Italian explorer from Florence who first realized that the West Indies were not, as Christopher Columbus had proclaimed, the edge of Asia but a whole new world. That is why the Americas, North and South, are named after the Latin version of Amerigo's first name: Americus."

Yep. Storm could be boring even in the middle of a chase scene.

Suddenly, Dad was in our earpieces too. "Hang on, Bick and Beck. Tommy and I borrowed a pair of Vespas."

"How'd you get out of the chains?" I just had to know.

"Simple trick I learned by studying the escape artistry of one Harry Houdini," said Dad matter-of-factly. "I'll teach you some day. After we recover this Egyptian treasure!"

In case you haven't figured it out, both our

parents are supersmart and have wicked mad skills.

"Here comes Mom!" said Beck. She had lifted up the back flap on the bad guys' getaway truck.

This was about to get interesting. Fast.

Hey, with us Kidds, things usually do!

CHAPTER 5

The musclemen driving the fake olive-oil truck must've realized Mom was on their tail.

All of a sudden, we were making incredibly sharp twists and turns, winding all over Florence. I pulled up the side tarp and saw the terra-cotta brick dome of the cathedral. I also saw a bunch of other orange-brown clay roofs whoosh past. The skyline of Florence made me remember how ancient this city is—more than two thousand years old!

But no matter how many side streets and

alleys the bad guys darted down, they couldn't shake Mom, the cops, or the Carabinieri a Firenze—the military police of Florence.

With our iPhones stuffed in our back pockets, Beck and I had become human tracking devices!

"Attenzione!" shouted the guy in the passenger seat. *"Pazzo americano!"*

Suddenly, the metal floor of the truck bed started to sizzle and spark with *zizz*ing jolts of vibrating voltage. Beck and I shuddered some.

The driver shrieked like he'd just stuck his finger into an electric outlet. Our fake olive-oil truck skidded sideways and came to an abrupt stop.

Beck and I both shook our heads. Our fizzy brains felt frazzled but we were fine. Beck flipped up the canvas at the rear of the truck and hopped out.

"Cool," she said.

I hopped out behind her. Somehow, our olive-oil truck had ended up parked in the middle of an outdoor art gallery.

"It's the courtyard of the Uffizi," said Beck. "One of the oldest and most famous art museums in the world."

"An appropriate resting spot for the pharaoh's sarcophagus," said Dad, climbing off his motor scooter while the police hauled the two no-neck goons out of the front seat of the truck.

"Tomorrow," said Mom as she and Storm emerged from their chase van, "this priceless relic will complete its journey home to its rightful owners in Cairo."

"And we'll start our well-earned family

vacation," added Dad. "After I have a few words with those two." He nodded toward the art thieves.

"Hope we didn't fry you guys too bad," said Tommy, tucking his Taser back into its holster.

Yep. Tommy and Dad had basically stungunned the truck. That's why the metal had sizzled like that. It was also why my hair was sticking straight up.

I'm not vain or anything, but even I knew this wasn't a good look for me.

CHAPTER 6

The Egyptian ambassador to Italy helicoptered from Rome to Florence to take charge of returning the priceless antiquities to their proper home.

"We cannot thank you enough, Dr. and Mrs. Kidd," said the Egyptian ambassador.

"You're very welcome," said Mom.

"We sort of helped," added Tommy with a dimpled grin, probably because the ambassador had brought along his teenage daughter. Tommy was wiggling his eyebrows the way he always does whenever there is a pretty girl within fifteen feet. Make that *one hundred* feet.

"Then I thank you as well, young Thomas Kidd," said the ambassador.

"As do I, Thomas," said his daughter.

"Please—call me Tommy. Or Tom. Just make sure you call me." He jiggled his hand near his ear like it was a phone.

Dad cleared his throat. "Thomas?"

Tommy took the hint and put his hand down, but not without a wink at the girl.

The ambassador stepped forward to shake Dad's hand. "If there is ever anything I or my country can do for any of you…"

"Well, Farid, now that you mention it," said Dad, "there is one thing."

"Name it."

"We'd very much like to talk to the two gentlemen who were attempting to smuggle your treasures through Italy. I suspect they are both pawns in a much bigger chess game and conspiracy. But these two pawns might be able to lead us to the kings and queens."

"And those little horsey pieces too," said Tommy. "Those are my favorite."

The ambassador's daughter giggled. Storm rolled her eyes. Beck and I tried not to barf.

"Let me make a few phone calls," said the ambassador. "Arrange an interview between you and these two, as you say, pawns."

One hour later, me, Beck, Storm, Tommy, and Mom were sitting behind a one-way mirror watching Dad interview the two handcuffed art thieves.

"Do you work for the international art thief Dionysus Streckting?" asked Dad. "If so, you should know that my children recently put him out of business."

It's true. Streckting was a major criminal in the stolen-art world. We'd nailed him in Berlin while Dad was busy rescuing Mom in Cyprus.

But instead of being impressed, the two goons laughed.

"Streckting is nothing," said one.

"We treat him with fishes in his face," said the other.

"That means they disrespect Streckting," said Storm, who had memorized all sorts of obscure Italian expressions on the flight to Florence.

The first goon's smile widened. His teeth (the ones he still had) looked like they were dripping black tar. "I feel sorry for you, Professor Dr. Kidd. You have no idea who or what you are dealing with."

That might've been true. But I had a feeling we were about to find out.

CHAPTER 7

The grinning goon leaned forward.

"Tell me, Professor, have you ever heard of the Enlightened Ones?" He rapped his knuckles on the table.

"I have heard certain rumors about a shadowy group of criminal conspirators who call themselves the Enlightened Ones," said Dad, cool as a cucumber.

The bad guy balled up his fist.

"It is no rumor, Professor. They are very, very real. As real as the ink in my skin."

"You cannot work for the Enlightened Ones unless you take a vow," added his colleague. "And get your knuckles tattooed. That'll hurt."

"What sort of vow?" asked Dad.

"*Omertà*," said the tough guy. "A code of silence. We will tell you nothing. We swear this on our honor."

"Interesting," said Dad with a slight grin. "I always heard there was no honor among thieves."

"You heard wrong, *signore!*"

"Do not worry, Professor," sneered knuckle man. "Even though we two will remain mute, you might soon hear from the Enlightened Ones themselves. They are professors and *intellettuali*, much like you. They like to play, how you say, mind games. It is very amusing for them to toy with eggheads and do-gooders. So keep your eyes and ears open, Dr. Thomas Kidd. We will tell you nothing. But the Enlightened Ones? Who knows? They may soon drop you a very clever clue."

After about thirty more minutes of questions, very few answers, and all sorts of tattooed-knuckle table knocking, Dad wrapped things up with the two pawns and came into the observation room to join us.

"Their code of silence is unshakable," he said. "They're not going to tell us anything."

"Most likely because the repercussions if they did would be severe," said Storm, slicing her finger across her throat like a dagger. Yep, Storm can be kind of blunt like that. But we love her anyway.

"Who are these Enlightened Ones?" I asked.

Dad turned to his daughter with the photographic memory. "Storm?"

BRAIN IN PROGRESS!

63%

Storm cocked her left eyebrow and waited a half a second. That's the look she gets on her face whenever she's flipping through the random-access memory device in her ginormous brain.

"The Enlightened Ones are rumored to be a small band of criminal masterminds and art thieves," said Storm. "They consider themselves the new Medicis. The Medicis, of course, were a powerful family who lived here in Florence centuries ago. They sponsored Renaissance artists and therefore owned the most spectacular collection of paintings, sculptures, and art objects in the world. But unlike the Medici family, who paid for the art, the Enlightened Ones prefer to *steal* their masterpieces."

Dad and Mom were nodding.

"Remember that list of the world's greatest unfound treasures that I used to keep in the Room on the *Lost*?" asked Dad. "I've often feared that this mysterious underground group of master art thieves might've already found a few of them."

"You mean things like the missing Kruger millions, the lost Fabergé eggs, and King John the Bad's treasure?" I blurted.

"That's right, Bick. If the Enlightened Ones are real, they might very well be hoarding treasure worth billions and billions of dollars in some top secret hidden location. They might also be actively hunting more treasure."

"Then we need to get busy," said Tommy. "Beat them to the punch! Find the rest of those super-treasures before they do."

"Exactly," said Dad. He glanced at his dive watch. "Anybody else hungry? I'm in the mood for those eggs Bick just mentioned."

"Yes!" Beck and I said with a double arm-pump. Dad wasn't talking about a late-night snack. He meant we were going on another treasure hunt: to find the lost Fabergé eggs!

"Next stop, Russia," said Dad. "This family has definitely earned a vacation. And vacations are always more fun when you spend them together...hunting treasure!"

CHAPTER 8

We jetted north to Russia.
Saint Petersburg, to be exact.

"Saint Petersburg is the second-largest city in all of Russia," said Storm on our taxi ride into the city. "It is located on the Baltic Sea's Gulf of Finland."

Tommy scratched his head. "I thought we were in Russia, not Finland."

"Tommy, did you keep up with your geography homework while I was being held hostage in Cyprus?"

"Chya. Of course I did, Mom."

She gave him her patented you're-not-fooling-me look. It's like a superpower that only moms have.

Feeling the force of it, Tommy glanced down. "A little. Some."

Mom kept giving him her look.

"Okay, not at all," Tommy admitted sheepishly. "Sorry. My bad."

"Well, Thomas," said Dad, "there's no better way to learn about geography than to actually visit the landmasses and seas you are studying."

"Um," I said, "I thought this was supposed to be our summer *vacation?*"

"It is. Nine whole days. But that doesn't mean our brains need to take a break too."

"Actually," said Beck, "in America, kids get, like, two or three whole months off."

"They play a lot of video games over the summer," I added. "Then they ride their bikes, go swimming, go to camp, play some more video games, and eat a ton of hot dogs, toasted marshmallows, and ice cream."

"A couple of them read too," said Storm. "The ones with good summer-reading programs."

"If you ask me," said Dad, "summer vacations at American schools are far too long. Three months? That's ridiculous. It might be the reason so many American kids forget everything they've learned during the school year."

"Summer vacation can also create bad work habits," said Mom.

"Like what?" asked Beck, who was sketching the onion-like domed roof of the Cathedral of the Resurrection, the coolest building in all of Saint Petersburg.

"There's no structure," said Mom. "No routine.

Summer vacations are just too loosey-goosey."

Yep. That's our mom and dad. Even though our constant globe-trotting meant we couldn't attend a real school, they always made sure we were keeping up with our studies.

"So, even though we're on vacation," announced Dad, "there will be no Kidd family summer slide. We've hired a tour guide and tutor for our time in Russia. Ah, there she is." He tapped on the divider window to get the taxi driver's attention. *"Pozhaluysta, ostanovite zdes',"* said Dad.

The cab came to a stop in front of that awesome cathedral.

"Spasibo," Dad said to the driver. "Come on, Kidds. This is going to be our best, most exciting summer ever!"

We stepped out of the cab and met our tutor, Larissa Bukova.

The second Tommy saw her, I'm pretty sure he started having *his* best summer ever.

CHAPTER 9

After touring the cathedral, we visited the Grand Palace, Palace Square, the Winter Palace, and the Catherine Palace.

Yep. There are a lot of palaces in Saint Petersburg, and Larissa Bukova told us absolutely everything about each and every one of them.

"The Catherine Palace, built in the flamboyant rococo style, was the summer residence of the Russian czars..."

Blah-blah-blah.

Mom and Dad were soaking it up. Tommy too. He was definitely falling hard for Larissa Bukova (that's one of the reasons Mom and Dad call him

Tailspin Tommy—he nosedives into a love spiral every time he meets a new girl).

Storm, however, did not seem happy. In fact, I had never seen her look so sad.

Larissa Bukova's knowledge of Saint Petersburg, and everything else (including how to make Herring under Fur Coat, a Russian dish with layers of salted herring and cooked vegetables topped off with a frosting of grated beets mixed with mayo), totally dwarfed Storm's knowledge, which we'd all thought was undwarfable.

"The Catherine Palace was also the last known location of the Amber Room, which was built in the early 1700s," said Dad with a sigh. "It disappeared in World War Two."

"Yes," said Larissa. "I was just about to mention that."

"Me too," said Storm.

Larissa kept going. "The Amber Room was so named because it was lined with panels decorated with six tons of amber and gold, and it was considered the Eighth Wonder of the World. We suspect the Nazis took the room's priceless panels back to Germany during World War Two, but they have never been found."

Dad nodded and stroked his chin.

I wondered if he was thinking the same thing I was: Had the Enlightened Ones found the stolen panels from the Amber Room? Did they have a headquarters with a ballroom made out of gold-encrusted amber walls?

Only one thing was certain: Dad's treasure-hunting brain never, *ever* went on vacation.

We left the Catherine Palace and moved on to the Hermitage Museum. Larissa Bukova, of course, went with us. Beck started calling her Krazy Glue because we couldn't shake her. I didn't like how sad she was making Storm feel by stealing all her thunder.

"The Hermitage has more paintings than any museum in the world," said Larissa.

"Russian emperors used to live here," said Storm.

"The museum opened in 1852," Larissa shot back.

"Admission is free on the first Thursday of every month!" yelled Storm.

Yep. They were having a nerd-off.

"Larissa," Dad cut in, "I was wondering—can you take us to the Fabergé Museum? I am very interested in the Easter eggs."

"I can take you there," blurted Storm. "I've already mapped out the shortest route in my head."

"Wonderful," said Mom. "Lead the way, Stephanie."

Yay, Mom. She could tell Storm was feeling bummed too.

CHAPTER 10

The Fabergé Museum's top attraction?

Nine priceless Easter eggs.

"Only fifty imperial eggs were ever made," reported Larissa Bukova. "And they were crafted right here in Saint Petersburg by the jeweler to the czars, Carl Fabergé!"

"Was he, like, the jeweler to the stars in Hollywood too?" said Tommy, trying to be charming.

"No," said Larissa. "He was Russian. All of those fifty bejeweled eggs were given as Easter gifts by the last two czars to their wives and mothers."

Larissa and Storm led us to a display case filled with the sparkling, fantastical eggs.

"How much are these baubles worth?" asked Beck.

"In 2004," said Larissa, "Viktor Vekselberg, one of Russia's wealthiest business tycoons, purchased these nine eggs for one hundred million dollars."

"Whoa," said Tommy, adding an impressed

whistle. "That's like eleven million dollars an egg."

"And," I added, "he didn't even bring home a whole dozen."

Tommy and I fist-bumped on that.

When we did, a very stern-looking little lady marched over to have a word with us. So far in Russia, all the museum guards had been older women. They didn't wear uniforms. They didn't need to. They looked scary enough without them.

"Are you, by any chance, Professor Thomas Kidd?"

We all stared at her in surprise.

Except for Dad. He'd been around long enough to expect the unexpected. *"Da,"* he said seriously.

"This, then, is for you."

She stiffly handed Dad a sealed envelope.

"Spasibo," said Dad. "Thank you."

She sniffed and eyed Tommy. "No more whistling," she said, wagging her finger at Tommy.

Then she turned on her heel and, shoes clicking, walked out of the gallery.

I checked out the envelope in Dad's hand and gasped.

It was sealed with wax. And stamped in the middle of the seal was a symbol I recognized!

CHAPTER 11

Dad carefully slid open the envelope and removed the crisp notecard tucked inside.

Then he, Mom, and Storm studied it.

(Well, with Storm, it was more like she was scanning it into her photographic memory for permanent storage.)

"Do you need help translating the message?" asked the ever-helpful brainiac Larissa Bukova. "I speak fourteen different languages fluently."

"Is that all?" scoffed Storm. "Relax, Comrade. It's in English. I think I can handle it."

"What the heck is it?" I asked. "Some kind of secret message?"

"Not exactly," said Mom.

"I believe it's a challenge," added Dad.

"This is just what those flunkies in Florence told us might happen," said Storm. After taking half a second to rewind the digital tape in her enormous brain, she quoted: "'Keep your eyes and ears open, Dr. Thomas Kidd. We will tell you nothing. But the Enlightened Ones? Who knows? They may soon drop you a very clever clue.'"

Wow. We'd just been handed our first clue to—well, *something*!

"So what'd they tell us?" asked Beck. "Is it about one of the missing treasures?"

"Do they have the rest of the Fabergé eggs?" asked Tommy.

I jumped in too. "Did they tell you where they stashed the Amber Room? Because they'd need a really big storage space to hide that."

"Like they would tell us that in a clue," Beck said.

"How do you know?" I snapped.

"Because that would be dumb, like you!"

"You mean dumb like *you!*"

51

Yes, we were about to launch into one of our famous Twin Tirades. This would've been number 607.

But we didn't. Mom and Dad were kind of glaring at us so we backed off.

"We'll all need to focus to solve these clues," Mom said.

"This is an extremely important hunt, guys," said Dad. "Whatever this treasure is, if we can manage to find it, it belongs to the world."

"We'll find it, Dad!" Tommy said.

"Piece of cake!" said Storm.

Mom looked at me and Beck. "How about you two?"

Beck and I looked at each other and nodded. "We're in," we said together.

Because that's what twins do.

CHAPTER 12

Dad clapped his hands and rubbed them together the way he did when it was time to pull in the lines on the boat and shove off. "Okay, Kidds, we have work to do."

I raised my hand. "Um, I thought we were supposed to be on our summer vacation."

"We were," said Mom, glancing at her watch. "For thirty-six hours."

"You're counting the flight from Florence?"

"They served you soft drinks and snacks, didn't they?"

"Yeah, but—"

Mom went on. "Do you have soft drinks and snacks every day?"

"No. Only on vacation."

"I rest my case," she said with a smile.

Dad turned to Mom with one of those looks that says a lot without saying anything. "Sue?"

Mom just nodded, "I agree, Thomas."

"I'll leave tonight."

Time for me to raise my hand again. "Um, what are you guys talking about?"

"Your father needs to take off," said Mom.

"Again?" said Beck. "We just found him, like, two weeks ago."

"This totally bites," added Tommy.

"Indeed it does," said Dad. "But I think these clues from the art thieves who call themselves the Enlightened Ones will eventually lead us to the biggest treasure ever, anywhere, at any time—their top secret lair of stolen treasure!"

"So why can't we come with you?" asked Beck.

"Yeah," said Tommy. "If this treasure is so big, you'll probably need help carrying it."

"Because," said Mom, "the five of us, with Larissa's assistance, need to work the puzzle *here*, in Russia. After all, the message was delivered to us in a Russian museum by a Russian museum guard."

"Which means," said Dad, "the Enlightened Ones are here in Saint Petersburg too!"

CHAPTER 13

We left the fancy-egg museum and headed to where we'd be spending our first night in Saint Petersburg: the State Hermitage Museum Official Hotel.

Yep. Our five-star accommodations were part of the art museum.

Dad and Mom went into their room and repacked Dad's bag so he could take off in search of the Enlightened Ones' treasure trove. I was guessing it was hidden inside an inactive volcano crater that could be reached only by submarine.

Then again, I'd just watched a James Bond movie on the flight up from Florence.

Storm set to work in her room poring over the clue that we received. Tommy was in the bathroom, busily scrunching his hair, something he hadn't done "in like six hours!"

That meant Beck and I were alone. In the living room.

Despite our truce from earlier, Twin Tirade 607 had been simmering for several hours. We were totally ready to blow.

Our tirades don't actually fit the dictionary definition of the word *tirade,* which Mom made us look up during one of our English lessons: "A long angry speech. A rant, diatribe, or harangue."

Our harangues never lasted very long. They were more like sparklers. We'd shoot off all sorts of hot and sizzling silver sparks from our red cores for maybe a minute. Then we'd fizzle out.

That day's tirade topic? Dad's plan to abandon ship.

Again.

Yes, Beck's skills are much more visual than verbal. As the writer in the family, I am much, much better at name-calling.

"I'll tell you who I am, you cantankerous contrarian. I am your awesome twin brother and the author of our family's adventure books."

"You also have a crusty booger inside your left nostril."

"Hey, you put that there!"

"Well, duh."

"It's very realistic-looking."

"I picked up some tips about playing with light and shadow from the grand masters' collection at the Hermitage art museum today."

"Oh. That's pretty impressive."

"Thanks."

"Um, what were we fighting about?"

"I forget."

"Yeah. Me too."

"Let's go help Storm with that clue."

"Cool."

And just like that, Twin Tirade 607 was done.

We headed into Storm's room to start work.

We were going to help Dad find the Enlightened Ones' world headquarters, no matter where it might be.

(I really hoped it was hidden inside a volcano crater! That would be so cool!)

And all we had to help us was the first clue, the one the museum guard handed to Dad:

WANT TO FIND OUR
SECRET TREASURE TROVE?

HERE IS A HINT, DR. KIDD:

It used to be the top of the world,
but time and a changing climate
changed that.

Even Storm was stumped. And if that's the case, you know this one's going to be a doozy.

CHAPTER 14

hat night, we said our good-byes to Dad.

"Make me proud, kids," said Dad.

"They will," said Mom.

"I'm going to miss you, Sue."

"I'll miss you too, Tom."

And then they hugged and kissed and junk. I tried not to watch.

Finally, Tommy cleared his throat. Mom and Dad knocked off all the mushy stuff.

"Um, you guys?" said Tommy. "Before Dad goes, we wanted to give him, uh, you know, something."

"It's a bon-voyage gift," I said, because Tommy

was sweating profusely. He always gets tongue-tied whenever he has to say anything semi-emotional. That's another reason we call him Tailspin Tommy.

I handed Dad a gift-wrapped box.

"We were going to give this to you next week, on your birthday, but since you may not be here, we figured we should give it to you now."

"What is it?" Dad asked as he tore off the wrapping paper.

"You could call it a replacement. For the one we tossed overboard off the coast of the Cayman Islands."

"We thought you were shark bait," blurted out Storm, who always says whatever's on her mind whenever it happens to show up there. Even if no one wants to hear it. "So we gave you a burial at sea."

"Without a body," added Tommy. "Because, you know, you and your body weren't there. Probably because you were, like, alive somewhere else..."

Dad took our gift, a brand-new captain's hat, out of the box and popped it on his head. He tugged down the brim to give it the jaunty angle he preferred.

"It was very moving. Even though I never actually thought you were dead," I said.

IT'S PERFECT. EVEN BETTER THAN THE OLD ONE.

"You'll keep in touch?" said Mom as Dad grabbed his duffel.

"Definitely." He turned his wrist to check his dive watch. "I need to take off. The secretary of state is letting me hitch a ride on his C-17 transport plane. Group hug?"

And the six of us formed a rugby scrum in the middle of the living room.

"I'll be fine," said Dad. "And I'll send you any clues I happen to pick up along the way!"

Great, because we could use all the help we could get!

CHAPTER 15

The next morning, we were sitting in the living room of our hotel suite eating the black bread, porridge, blini, and *oladyi*—which are served with butter, sour cream, jam, and caviar—brought up by room service for breakfast. We were watching *Good Morning, Russia* on the state-owned Channel One.

We don't usually watch much TV (we're too busy having adventures), but Mom told us TV could be a valuable tool when attempting to learn a new language.

I guess. I still didn't understand a word of what the giggly early-morning-TV people were saying or why they were dressed in aluminum foil.

Suddenly, a high-pitched beeping noise pierced all our eardrums.

"That's my secure line," said Mom, rummaging around inside her backpack.

She pulled out a pretty awesome-looking satellite phone. (I think Mom and Dad still get the CIA discount on all their supercool spy gear.)

"We're on our way," Mom said into her phone before she powered it down.

"What's going on?" I asked.

"There's been a burglary," she reported. "Next door. At the Hermitage art museum. Several masterpieces are missing—including a priceless Rembrandt."

"No!" gasped Beck. "Not the Rembrandt! He's my favorite!"

"Everybody go and grab your gear," said Mom.

"We're heading back to the museum."

"Do we have to pay the admission fee again?" asked Tommy.

"No, Tommy. We're going back as official consultants. The Russians know we're in town. They also know that, when it comes to finding stolen artworks, the Kidds are the best treasure hunters in the world!"

Larissa Bukova met us outside the Hermitage.

"It is a madhouse in there," she said. "This is the most horrible crime against the Russian state and people since 1980!"

"What happened way back then?" I asked.

"The amateur United States hockey team defeated the far superior Soviet Union national team at the Lake Placid Winter Olympics," said Larissa sourly.

"Woo-hoo!" shouted Tommy. Then he started pumping his fist in the air. "U.S.A.! U.S.A.!"

Mom arched an eyebrow. "Thomas? Remember where you are."

"Right. No patriotic fist-pumping allowed."

We hurried into the Hermitage. We were in the same wedding-cake room we'd been in the day before, only now the place was packed. I saw Russian police, reporters, tourists, the Russian army, and even Vladimir Putin.

A schlumpy little man in a trench coat waddled over to where we stood staring in horror at the blank spots on the walls. You could still see the outlines of the paintings that should've been hanging there.

"*Zdravstvuyte*," he said. "I am Inspector Gorky. You are the world-famous Kidds, no?"

"That's right," said Mom. "And this is our tutor, translator, and tour guide, Miss Larissa Bukova."

Tommy put his hand beside his mouth and whispered, "She's also a hottie."

Inspector Gorky clicked his heels and bowed slightly. "*Zdravstvuyte*, Miss Bukova. *Ne yavlyayutsya li eti americanskie 'ohotniki za sokrovishchami' na samom dele inostrannymi shpionami?*"

"No," said Storm, "we American treasure hunters are *not* foreign-espionage agents."

"If I may," asked Inspector Gorky, "where is your world-famous leader, the renowned art historian and treasure hunter Professor Thomas Kidd?"

"He was called away last night unexpectedly," said Mom.

Gorky cocked a skeptical eyebrow. "Last night? Unexpectedly?"

"Yeah," I said. "We weren't expecting it. Neither was he. It was like a surprise party but without any of the good stuff like ice cream or cake."

"I see," said Inspector Gorky. "Tell me, then, is Professor Kidd still working for, how you say, the Agency?"

"No," said Mom.

"Ah. Then who or what is he working for?"

"The good of humanity. Now then, Inspector," said Mom, nodding toward one of the blank spots on the wall, "I believe we have work to do. What did they take?"

The inspector pulled a spiral notebook out of the inside pocket of his rumpled trench coat and read a list.

"Leonardo da Vinci's *Madonna Litta, The Lute Player* by Caravaggio, Giorgione's *Judith*, and *Danaë* by Rembrandt."

"This is unbelievable," muttered Mom. "Thomas leaves to pursue the Enlightened Ones, and the very next day, this happens?"

"I'm sorry," said Inspector Gorky, "you were mumbling. I did not understand."

"Nothing," said Mom. "Just that this has to be one of the biggest art heists in history."

"Yes," said Inspector Gorky. "It is big. Very, very big."

Like Mom, I had a hunch that the despicable Enlightened Ones were somehow involved. They'd probably already submarined all four of the missing paintings to their secret volcano treasure vault.

That's why they sent Dad that coded clue.

They wanted the cat to go away so their sticky-fingered mice could come to the art museum and play.

And by *play*, I mean *steal!*

CHAPTER 16

Mom and Storm went over to examine the wall where some of the missing art used to hang. The rest of us sort of tagged along.

"We were just in this room yesterday," Mom said to Storm. "Notice anything different?"

"Give me a second."

Uh, the paintings are missing? Even I know that one.

"Okay," said Storm. "One—four priceless paintings are missing from the walls. Two—those potted flowers weren't here yesterday.

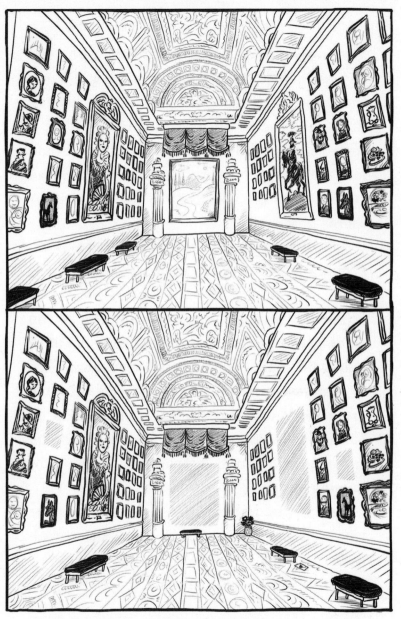

CAN YOU SPOT SIX THINGS THAT ARE DIFFERENT? STORM CAN!

Three—somebody painted a mustache on the guy on the bottom row near the horse. Four— the horse paintings have been switched around. Five—the benches have been rearranged. Six— somebody dropped an envelope with a wax seal, identical to the envelope the guard handed Dad yesterday, on the floor next to that bench over there."

"The Enlightened Ones!" I whispered to Beck. I could see the waxy red splotch from ten yards away.

Tommy was heading over to pick it up when the strangest thing happened: A kid in a long fur coat (even though it was the middle of summer) and sunglasses strode into the art gallery with two Russian wolfhounds on leashes. He was maybe thirteen years old and surrounded by six bodyguards, their muscles bulging under tight business suits.

He stopped in front of Tommy, blocking the way to the envelope. "Do not trouble yourself with the trash," he said to my brother. "I pay people to pick things up for me."

Before Tommy could answer, the young teen-ager snapped his fingers. One of his bodyguards scurried over, scooped up the envelope, and tucked it into his pocket without, of course, showing it to us.

"May we see that?" asked Mom.

"No," said the kid in the fur coat. "You may not."

"But it may be evidence."

"And it may be *musor*."

"That's 'trash, rubbish, or litter,'" translated Storm.

Mom put her hands on her hips. You know how Storm gets super-mad sometimes? Guess where she learned it?

"And who, exactly, are you?" demanded Mom.

"He is Viktor Zolin," said Inspector Gorky. "One of our most eccentric and generous Russian billionaires. He is only thirteen."

"*Da,*" said Zolin, "this is true. But for your information, Inspector Gorky, I will be *fourteen* in three months. I also donate many rubles, euros, and dollars to this marvelous museum."

"It is why we let him bring his dogs," added Gorky.

Zolin marched forward and stared at the blank spots on the walls.

"No!" he exclaimed. "They told me what had happened but I refused to believe them. Now I see it for myself and I find my soul filled with the same dread, despair, and remorse that so many brooding Russians feel in our many depressing novels and stage plays. This is too, too cruel. Such beauty has been stolen from us? How can this possibly be?"

"Easy there, cowboy," said Storm, the girl with no filter between her brain and her mouth. "Some bad guys busted in and ripped paintings off the walls. We'll get them back. Now, if you'll give us that clue your stump-necked muscleman just snatched off the floor—"

Zolin held up his hand to silence Storm.

"No. First I must weep. I must weep and mourn Mother Russia's loss!"

And so he wept.

Then his bodyguards wept.

And then the pair of wolfhounds started howling.

Viktor Zolin dried his eyes with a silk handkerchief. He blew his nose in another silk handkerchief. Then he dabbed his eyes with a fresh hankie. The guy pulled out so many different-colored silks, he reminded me of a magician. At last, he took a deep breath, spun around, and scowled at us.

"How could your horrible husband do this to us?" he screamed at Mom.

What?

"I beg your pardon?" (That's my mom's polite way of saying *"What?"*)

"I know where Dr. Thomas Kidd went last night!" Zolin shouted. "He came here to the Hermitage to steal our beloved national treasures, then he fled the country like a snake! But he made one terrible mistake—leaving his family behind to take the fall. Arrest these greedy American thieves! Arrest them immediately!"

The nearby Russian soldiers, who were armed to the teeth, drew their weapons and lunged forward like the witch's guards in *The Wizard of Oz*. They had us surrounded!

Did they think we had the stolen da Vinci and Caravaggio in our backpacks?

"You're making a mistake!" cried Mom as my wrists were pulled behind me and locked together with plastic zip ties. I saw Tommy struggle against the army guards but there were too many of them.

82

"Where is your husband, Mrs. Kidd?" demanded Inspector Gorky.

"I...I...I don't really know," Mom said.

"Where was he last night?"

"He went away. On a mission."

"Da!" snapped Viktor Zolin. "A *burglary* mission! Soldiers, take the Kidd family and their double-agent tutor-spy out of here! Lock them up! Throw away the key! Dr. Thomas Kidd has stolen our priceless national treasures. For this, his wife, children, and hired help must pay!"

I couldn't believe what was happening even as they dragged us out of the museum and into police vans.

The Russians thought Dad had stolen their priceless and precious artwork?

He would never, ever do that.

Or would he?

CHAPTER 17

Did Dad really steal the paintings from the Hermitage like the weepy Viktor Zolin said he had?

I'd have a lot of time to ponder this question (and many more) because the six of us were thrown into jail with no one around who could help us.

It was the kind of dark, dank, and dingy prison where you can't do much besides ponder, think, brood, and, generally, get stinky.

"Russia is famous for its brutal prisons," said

Larissa because, I guess, she never quit being a tour guide. "This place is nothing compared to Petak Island, the most isolated prison in all of Russia. There, inmates spend twenty-two hours a day in their cells, pace about in a cramped outdoor cage during yard time, and can receive parcels and packages only twice each year."

Larissa kept going. "Then there is the high-security Black Dolphin Prison near the Kazakhstan border, where prisoners are blindfolded when they arrive and whenever they leave their cells so they cannot memorize the layout and plan escapes."

We were all getting kind of queasy but Larissa kept babbling on.

"Of course, there is also the notorious Lefortovo in Moscow, long a favorite of the KGB for, how you say, 'enhanced interrogations.' A dreaded place of isolation, torment, agony, torture, and pain—"

"Enough!" shouted Mom. "Stick a sock in it, Larissa. School is out for the day. Tour time is over."

"But—"

"*Tishe!* Be quiet!"

87

"As you wish, Madame Kidd. I will no longer enlighten you with fun facts to know and tell—"

"Larissa? You're still talking."

"This is true. I am, indeed, talking. Blabbing and blah-blah-blahing, as you Americans might—"

"Shh! Not one more word. Not a single peep-ski," growled Mom.

And, believe it or not, this finally shut Larissa Bukova up.

For about ten seconds.

"These iron bars," she said then, moving on to geography, "were most likely manufactured in Magnitogorsk, an industrial city in Chelyabinsk nestled at the base of the Ural Mountains..."

The rest of us jammed our fingers into our ears.

Until Mom's watch started chirping.

CHAPTER 18

"What, may I ask, is that chirping?" inquired Larissa.

"Papa Bird," said Mom excitedly.

Tommy and I shuffled down to the other side of our cell so we could be closer to Mom, Beck, and Storm.

"Good thing they didn't confiscate your watch," Beck whispered to Mom.

Mom nodded. "Yes. I wondered about that. Very lax security."

"Chya," said Tommy. "Especially given all

that junk Larissa was telling us about Russian prisons and how awful they are—"

"What are you Kidds blabbing about down there?" called Larissa, because we were all speaking so softly she couldn't make out a word we were saying. "I am the designated blabbermouth. What do you speak of in such hushed tones?"

"Um, this bird," I said. "It must've flown in through a window or something."

"Impossible," said Larissa. "This prison has no windows. It is a bleak and soulless place without light or a shred of hope."

"Um, maybe it's a pet of one of the guards."

"This is possible," said Larissa. "Is it a parrot?"

"Uh, yeah," I said, shrugging to everybody who was staring at me while I fibbed my head off. "A parrot."

Finally, Storm helped me out. *"Polli khochet kryeker?"* she squawked in her best Russian-parrot voice.

"A very smart bird," said Larissa because, in the darkness of the prison cells, she didn't realize the parrot was actually our big sister saying "Polly wants a cracker" in Russian.

Our tour guide/tutor launched into another fact-filled, boring monologue. "Many Russians enjoy spending time with domesticated animals. Parrots, cats, dogs, ferrets, mini-pigs, chinchillas, hedgehogs, decorative fish…"

Her blathering gave us the cover we needed for Mom to tell us what was up with her fancy spy-watch/communicator bit.

"I'm sure none of you think your father would steal the art and then leave us here," said Mom, looking at each of us in turn.

I didn't say anything, even though I had been wondering that.

"But in case you do, Dad was nowhere near the museum last night," whispered Mom as we all stared at the screen of her superwatch. "His tracking app just updated his status. He departed Russian airspace thirty minutes after he left our hotel room. He is now in Washington, DC."

"So why would Inspector Gorky and that billionaire kid Zolin say Dad stole all that stuff?" I asked, feeling guilty that I'd doubted him, even for a second.

"So the real thieves could get away," said Mom with a determined look in her eye.

"The Enlightened Ones!" blurted out Storm.

"Shh!" said everybody else, because we didn't want Larissa to stop her pet lecture at the far end of the cell block.

"We know the E-Ones have minions here in Saint Petersburg," whispered Mom.

"The little dudes from the movies?" asked Tommy. "I love them!"

Storm rolled her eyes. "*Minions* means 'henchmen.'"

"Chya, I knew that."

"Guys, remember who picked the clue up off the floor?" said Beck.

"Yes," said Storm, because, like I said, she remembers everything. "Viktor Zolin's bodyguard."

"Zolin is an Enlightened One!" I exclaimed as quietly as I could.

"But why would he pick up his own gang's clue?" asked Tommy.

Mom looked thoughtful. "Maybe he is trying to earn membership in their private club by helping to orchestrate the theft of four priceless paintings that they can add to their already impressive collection."

"Wait a second," said Beck. "He'd steal paintings from a museum he donates a ton of money to?"

"He might," said Mom. "Especially if he wanted access to the most exclusive art museum in the world: the secret society's treasure trove!"

"So why point the finger at us?" asked Tommy, who looked more confused than usual.

"We're the red herring," said Storm.

"We're smoked fish?" said Tommy. "Because I tasted that salty pink stuff at breakfast this morning and it was seriously disgusting."

"A red herring," said Mom patiently, "is something that's intended to be misleading or distracting. By hiding the clue and framing us for the theft, Zolin successfully threw the police off the trail of the real thieves."

"Plus," I added, "he gave the crooks a head start!"

Beck slumped to the floor. "And the stolen art is getting farther and farther away."

"But where are they taking it?" asked Tommy.

I snapped my fingers. "The volcano!"

"Whuh?"

"Sorry. That's where I think the Enlightened Ones have their top secret treasure lair."

"Seriously?" said Beck. "That's the dumbest idea you've ever come up with. What if the volcano erupts?"

I might've defended myself but Mom's watch started beeping and dinging.

That Dad-tracker app?

It was flashing with a red alert.

She swiped it sideways to reveal a very familiar face.

CHAPTER 19

"Just what we don't need," muttered Mom.

"What is it?" I asked.

"The correct question," said Mom, "is, *Who* is it?"

"Okay," said Tommy. "I've got this one, guys. Who is it, Mom?"

"Your uncle Timothy."

Quick background: Uncle Timothy (who isn't really our uncle) was Dad's handler when he was in the CIA. Uncle Timothy pretended to be our legal guardian when Mom was kidnapped and

Dad disappeared over the side of the *Lost*, our family's treasure-hunting boat. Then Uncle Timmy totally tortured us—he made us go to school for the first time ever! After that, he basically stole the treasure we needed to ransom Mom. Then Uncle T went complete double agent on everybody and tried to kill us, first in China and then Germany.

You can probably tell he's not our favorite person.

After his stunts in China and Germany, Uncle T was locked up in the most secure federal penitentiary in America: ADX Florence, the Alcatraz of the Rockies, in Colorado. It's a super-max prison. The cell furniture is just a desk, a stool, and a bed—all of them made out of poured concrete. The pillows are probably filled with pebbles. There are fourteen hundred remote-controlled steel doors, twelve-foot-high razor-wire fences, all sorts of laser-beam motion detectors, and an army of attack dogs.

ADX Florence made our Russian jail look like the Ritz.

But the most important thing about it is that no prisoner has ever escaped from the super-maximum-security facility in Colorado.

Except, somehow, Uncle Timothy did.

That's what the red alert on Mom's watch was all about.

"The wolf is on the prowl," whispered Mom when she finished reading the coded intel on her wrist.

My guess? Uncle Timothy was on his way to

Russia so he could steal the stolen art ten seconds after we Kidds recovered it. He probably planned to swoop in like a vulture and snatch it away.

Vulture action is what this particular wolf does best.

CHAPTER 20

Surprise, surprise.

Two minutes after Mom received the bulletin about Uncle Timothy's daring escape (apparently—and no one's exactly sure how he pulled this off—he'd found a way to flush himself down the toilet), Inspector Gorky paid us a visit in our jail cell.

"Greetings, American Kidd family," he said.

"Hello, Inspector," said Mom politely. "What brings you down here to our dungeon?"

"Most likely the Saint Petersburg Metro," said Larissa, because some tour guides never shut up. "It is the deepest subway system in the world, and the fare for a single journey to anywhere in the city, including this jail, is about one American dollar."

"They still use tokens, or *zhetons,* the size of large coins," added Storm, because she was still in that nerd-off with Larissa.

Inspector Gorky rolled his eyes.

"Guards?" he called out. "Kindly escort Miss Bukova to a different cell. One that is far from here."

"B-b-but—"

"It will give you more to talk about on your next guided tour!"

A pair of prison guards came and hauled Larissa away.

"You're not going to hurt her, are you?" demanded Mom after Larissa was gone.

"No," said Gorky. "I simply wish to prevent her from hurting my ears. Now then, you are, I am given to understand, treasure hunters?"

"Chya," said Tommy. "Only like the best in the world."

"Ah. So you can shoe a flea."

"Huh?"

"That's another Russian expression, Tommy," explained Storm. "It means we're talented."

"Oh. Okay. That's cool. Thought he was saying we had fleas."

"I need your help," said Gorky. "I do not trust billionaires. They will hang noodles on your ears."

We all looked to Storm.

"That means they'll lie to you."

"Just so," said Inspector Gorky. "Now then, from what my colleagues at the SVR, our Russian intelligence agency, tell me, you Kidd Family Treasure Hunters are used to deciphering clues? You can find a needle when one is sewing in a haystack, *da*?"

"What've you got?" asked Mom, trying to cut to the chase.

"Something I did not want Miss Bukova to see or hear."

The inspector explained that he'd seen Viktor Zolin's flunky snatch the clue envelope off the floor in the museum.

"Later," Gorky went on, "when the bodyguard was scooping up a pile of dog poop from the museum's marble floor, the envelope slipped out of his coat pocket. I picked it up before he realized he had dropped it. Being an inspector, I decided to inspect it. I broke the seal, memorized the message, and dropped the envelope back on the floor."

"Did the guard pick up the envelope again?" asked Mom.

"Yes."

"Um, didn't he think it was kind of suspicious that the wax seal was broken?" asked Beck.

"No," said Gorky. "He assumed it cracked open when it hit the hard marble floor."

"Seriously?"

Gorky shrugged. "He is a muscle-head, *da*?"

"The wax seal," I asked, "was there an E and a one stamped into it?"

"*Da*. How did you know this, youngest male Kidd?"

I puffed up my chest a little. "Like you said, Mr. Gorky. We're treasure hunters. We know stuff."

"What did the message say?" asked Beck.

"It was very strange. And in English too. I wrote it down."

And Inspector Gorky handed us the second clue to the whereabouts of the Enlightened Ones' secret treasure trove.

Mom immediately tapped it into her smart-watch and sent it to Dad.

And now, we'll give it to you.

SEARCHING FOR OUR SECRET TREASURE TROVE?

HERE IS ANOTHER HINT:

Approach from the south and you will see northern lights high up in the sky.

CHAPTER 21

"**D**oes this message mean anything to you?" asked Inspector Gorky.

"Yes," said Mom. "Whoever wrote this is familiar with the phenomenon known as the northern lights or, more exactly, the aurora borealis—a natural light show high in the sky over the magnetic North Pole."

"What does that have to do with—" the inspector started.

"Not to be confused with the aurora australis," cut in Storm, "which takes place in the Southern Hemisphere."

"Because that's where Australia is," said Tommy. "We're going to go there someday."

"I do not understand," said Inspector Gorky.

"Well," said Tommy, "Mom and Dad promised that we'd sail around the world, and since Australia is on the globe—"

"*Nyet!* The clue! What does it mean?"

"Simple," said Storm (probably because Larissa Bukova wasn't there to answer first). "If you approach from the south in a high-latitude Arctic region, you will see, in the north, the brilliant dancing lights of the aurora borealis. The lights are actually collisions between electrically charged particles from the sun that enter the Earth's atmosphere. The 'aurora' part of the name comes from the Roman goddess of dawn and—"

"*Perestan'!*" cried Inspector Gorky, tugging at the hair on both sides of his head. "*Vy svodite menya s uma!*"

"Well, I'm sorry," said Storm. "We don't mean to drive you mad—"

"You Kidds are worse than that billionaire brat Viktor Zolin."

"No way," said Tommy. "That dude's totally weepy."

"And his wolfhounds need a bath," added Beck. "They smell like wet fur."

"No," I said, "I think that was Zolin's coat—"

"Grrr! I've had enough of you impossible Americans!"

Inspector Gorky stomped away.

Which was exactly what we wanted him to do.

WAIT, I HAVEN'T TOLD YOU WHERE THE WORD "BOREALIS" COMES FROM. IT'S FROM THE GREEK NAME FOR THE GOD OF THE NORTH WIND, BOREAS.

WHICH IS WHAT YOU SHOULD BE CALLED BECAUSE YOU ARE A BORING WINDBAG!

"Family meeting," said Mom when we were (finally) alone. "We have two clues. What do you guys think they mean?"

"Um, what were they again?" asked Tommy.

Mom turned to Storm, who recited both clues from memory.

"One: It used to be the top of the world, but time and a changing climate changed that. Two: Approach from the south and you will see northern lights high up in the sky."

"The North Pole!" blurted Beck.

"Yeah," I said eagerly, "if you approach the North Pole from the south, you'll see the northern lights high up in the sky!"

Beck and I looked to Mom.

"You guys might be onto something," she said.

"Whoa," said Tommy. "You think the Enlightened Ones have stashed all their stolen art up at the North Pole?"

"Perhaps they put all their treasures into cold storage," said Storm with a rare grin. (Lately, she'd been cracking puns and we'd been wishing she'd stop.)

"Or," I said, "it could be like Superman's Fortress of Solitude. An ice castle located in a polar wasteland; an underground warehouse in the belly of a glacier!"

Mom arched an eyebrow. "Did you read a lot of comic books while I was being held by the kidnappers, Bick?"

"A few."

"What do you think, Mom?" asked Beck eagerly. "Did the bad guys take the stolen Russian art all the way to the North Pole?"

"It's a possibility," answered Mom. "One I'm willing to explore."

"Too bad we can't," said Storm bluntly. She shook the bars of her jail cell. "We're not exploring anywhere anytime soon."

That's when a furious Larissa Bukova came marching down the hall, escorted by a whole troop of prison guards.

"What did you fools say to Inspector Gorky?" she demanded.

"Just that we were missing you," said Tommy, wiggling his eyebrows.

"Well, congratulations, Thomas. We are all to be together again. In a new prison. The notorious Lefortovo in Moscow!"

I raised my hand. "Um, is that the one where the KGB used to torture people?"

"*Da!*"

I was afraid of that.

CHAPTER 22

*A*nd so we were moved.

They put us in a train car. I think the previous passengers had been a herd of cows.

No one told us exactly why we were being transported south to Moscow. Nobody gave us any explanations.

"It is the Russian way," Larissa said stoically, which is how a lot of Russians say stuff. They figure life's ups and downs (mostly downs) are just part of your destiny and there's nothing you can do to change it, so you just have to be tough and slog through it without complaining. Stoically.

"This stinks," said Tommy, and he didn't mean the cattle car. "I refuse to, you know, just accept that if my life sucks there's nothing I can do about it."

Being raised on the *Lost*, we were all taught that we were the masters of our own destinies. That we could do and be anything we wanted to do or be—as long as we worked at it hard enough.

Plus we complain a lot. We Kidds would've made terrible Russians.

So no way were we going to take our imprisonment lying down.

Especially not in a smellerific cattle car.

Surprisingly, when we arrived in Moscow, we weren't immediately sent to the dungeons of Lefortovo Prison.

Nope. We were sent someplace even worse: the Butyrka.

But, much to our surprise, we weren't tossed into another dark, dismal, and depressing dungeon.

"We just wanted to make sure you saw all the prisons included in your tour package," explained a very accommodating guard.

"This really is a tour?" I blurted out. "With the shackles and everything?"

"*Da,*" said Larissa. "One of our most popular tours. Right up there with the Red Army tour, where you get to visit Stalin's secret bunker and the Leningrad siege museum!"

"This way," said the guard. "We have prepared some light Russian refreshments."

"Now, if you please to finish your tea and refreshments," said the guard, "we will go see the Big Boss, who officially released you from the incarceration."

"The warden?" asked Mom.

"No," said the guard. "The Big Boss. The, how you say, head honcho. He is at the Kremlin."

"Whoa!" said Tommy. "We're going to see Vladimir Putin?"

"No. President Putin is busy wrestling a bear. You will see someone else. Please, eat your blintzes and blini quickly. We do not want to keep the big man waiting. He is easily angered."

Okay, this whole Russian adventure was becoming ridiculously scary—but also kind of scary-cool.

And the cheese blintzes with jam and sour cream?

Scary-delicious!

CHAPTER 23

We were whisked across town to the Kremlin in a luxurious ZiL limousine, the favorite ride of all Russian bigwigs.

And, of course, while we rode, Larissa Bukova and Storm had a fact-fight, telling us everything about the Kremlin that we never wanted to know.

During the ride, Mom told us all to be on our best behavior when we met the Big Boss, whoever he might be.

"We really want him to give us the resources to

head to the North Pole. It's a dangerous journey and we'll need a lot of supplies," she said.

"Do you think that's really where the Enlightened Ones have hidden all the stolen artwork?" I asked, because, to be honest, I was starting to have my doubts. (I hope you guys have come up with some other answers.)

"The clues sure seem to point that way," said Tommy.

"And Dad *seemed* to be dead when we were in that storm off the Cayman Islands," I said. "You can see the northern lights in Alaska—you don't have to go to the North Pole."

"But what about that top-of-the-world clue?" said Beck. "Where else could that be?"

"I don't know. Maybe there's a revolving restaurant in Las Vegas called the Top of the World." (Turns out I was right about that one.)

"Enough, you guys," said Mom. "Even if we are misreading the riddles, there is a lot of good we can do up in the Arctic Circle. Remember what Dad and I have always said: the greatest treasures in this world aren't made of gold, precious stones, or even paint on canvas."

Beck the art lover gasped a little when Mom said that last part.

(Come on, Beck. You know you did. You looked like you might have a heart attack.)

Our limo driver escorted us into the Kremlin and a very ornate meeting room, where the Big Boss was waiting for us.

"Please, sit down, Kidd Family Treasure Hunters," said a burly man in a business suit as he gestured toward some very plush chairs. "Allow me to introduce myself. I am Gage Szymanowicz, minister of emergency situations."

"Cool," said Tommy. "So when people call 911, are you the guy who answers?"

Mom cleared her throat. Shook her head.

Tommy blushed a little. "Sorry, sir. My bad."

"Actually," said the ever-unhelpful Larissa, "Mr. Szymanowicz's department's official name is Ministry of the Russian Federation for Affairs for Civil Defense, Emergencies, and Elimination of Consequences of Natural Disasters."

Szymanowicz gave Larissa Bukova the Russian stink-eye.

Snap! She shut right up—just like that! It was absolutely amazing. Szymanowicz definitely knew how to deal with natural disasters, including ones named Larissa.

"I am most alarmed by the art theft at the Hermitage in Saint Petersburg," said Minister Szymanowicz. "It is indeed a national emergency."

"We agree," said Mom. "And we'll do anything we can to help you recover your lost treasures."

"Except eat more of that meat-and-gelatin mold they served for lunch," said Storm. "That stuff was just gross."

"I apologize for your recent imprisonment," said Minister Szymanowicz, bowing slightly.

"We're just happy to be free," said Mom.

"We're Americans," added Tommy. "We're used to living that way."

Our Russian host pretended not to be insulted. "Tell me," he said, "where is Professor Thomas Kidd?"

"Away," said Mom. That's spy talk for *None of your business.*

"I am very disappointed your heroic husband is not here to help us in this hour of extreme national need."

"I'm sorry too," said Mom. "But, trust me, it was an emergency."

"Oh yes. I am certain it was. Where exactly did he go?" Szymanowicz pressed. Apparently, he didn't speak spy.

"He didn't tell me."

"Is that so? Is he searching for some other treasure?"

Mom grinned but she didn't answer.

Szymanowicz kept pushing. "Is anybody else searching for the same treasure your husband seeks?"

Mom was a pro at handling interrogations. She just kept on smiling. She didn't say a word, but her eyes said, *I ain't talking, pal. Move on.*

"So," said Minister Szymanowicz with an exasperated sigh, "can you at least tell me where you think we might find the purloined paintings?"

"Certainly," said Mom.

And everybody (except me) said: "The North Pole."

CHAPTER 24

"The North Pole?" said Gage Szymanowicz with a rumbling chuckle. "Do you suspect Santa Claus is the scoundrel who stole our missing masterpieces?"

"Minister," said Mom, trying to silence his laughter, "have you ever heard of a shadowy underground association whose members call themselves the Enlightened Ones?"

He shrugged. "I have heard the rumors, of course. They say the Enlightened Ones are a fiendish cartel of super-rich billionaires who are attempting to seize and hoard all of the world's greatest treasures. But I do not believe in these rumors, the same way I do not believe in Santa Claus or, as we Russians call him, Ded Moroz—Grandfather Frost."

"You don't believe?" said Tommy. "Did Grandfather Frost forget to bring you a bicycle or something one year?"

Mom shook her head again. "Thomas?"

"Sorry, sir. My bad. Again."

"The Enlightened Ones have been sending us clues pointing toward the North Pole as the hiding place for all their looted booty," said Storm. "It's almost like they're drawing us a treasure map made up of riddles instead of dotted lines."

"Is this so?" said Minister Szymanowicz, arching one bushy eyebrow.

"Well, that's one way to interpret the clues," I said.

Now Mom was giving *me* the stink-eye.

So I added, "And right now, it's probably the best way too."

"May I see these clues?"

"Only if you buy a copy of the book I'm going to write."

"Proshu proshcheniya? I beg your pardon?"

"We're putting the clues in the book we're doing about our adventures in Italy, Russia, and wherever else we end up on this treasure hunt," explained Beck. "When the book comes out, I'm sure you'll enjoy my drawings a ton more than Bick's writing."

"Will not," I countered.

"Will too."

"Won't."

"Will!"

Mom cleared her throat again. (She has to do that a lot when we're out in public.)

"Twins? Settle down. We don't have time for one of your tirades. We have art to rescue."

"This is true," said Minister Szymanowicz, getting back on track. "Now, how do they say this in the movies? Ah, yes. Your mission, should you choose to accept it, is to save art and, in so doing, save civilization. Without art and culture, what are we humans? Nothing but bumbling barbarians with no beauty in our lives! Even our prehistoric forefathers knew this. Why else would they decorate their cave walls with primitive paintings?" Szymanowicz asked.

"To be more specific," said Szymanowicz, "I want you, the Kidd Family Treasure Hunters, to go find the art that was stolen out of the Hermitage Museum in Saint Petersburg as well as the priceless paintings recently stolen from the Louvre in Paris, the Metropolitan Museum of Art in New York City, and the Saatchi Gallery in London. We are certain there is a connection among all these thefts."

Wow. That earned a collective gasp.

Who knew so many artistic treasures had gone missing?

Larissa Bukova, that's who. She launched into another one of her scholarly (make that *boring*) monologues.

"None of these thefts have ever been reported in the press. However, due to the superiority of our Russian intelligence agencies, our fearless leaders know all about them. For we are the champions of culture and civilization."

"This is very true, Larachka," said Minister Szymanowicz, smiling.

Weird. The way he said that, I got a funny feeling that the Russian minister of emergency-type stuff knew our tour guide.

But that wasn't possible.

Or was it?

CHAPTER 25

Minister Szymanowicz wasn't done with his plot-thickening ingredients.

"You were recommended for this job by the famous billionaire Viktor Zolin."

"The teenage weeper?" I blurted out.

"*Da.* Viktor is very emotional. He cries so much, he had to hire an extra bodyguard just to carry his tissue boxes."

"Wait a second," said Tommy. "Viktor Zolin is the one who told the cops to toss us in jail."

Minister Szymanowicz nodded. "As I said, he is very emotional. Prone to mood swings. We apologize for any inconvenience caused by your recent incarceration. I assure you that you were never suspects in this crime."

"Viktor Zolin is also worth several billion dollars," added Larissa Bukova. "Most of it has come from his family's oil and gas holdings. When his parents mysteriously died, young Viktor inherited everything."

"What do you mean, *mysteriously*?" asked Storm, who was probably pegging thirteen-year-old Viktor as a prime murder suspect.

"It was a freak accident," explained Larissa. "Viktor's parents were visiting an artistic installation known as the Ice Palace that was erected in Saint Petersburg ten years ago. Viktor, of course, was only three years old at the time so his parents left him with his *babushka*—his grandmother—while they explored the magnificent sculpture created by master ice artists using three tons of ice blocks chiseled out of nearby lakes. The frozen building was a replica of the original Ice Palace built in 1740 to celebrate the Russian victory in the Turkish war and honor the tenth anniversary of Empress Anna's reign. It was nearly thirty feet tall and incredibly beautiful."

"So what happened?" I asked Larissa.

"The sun came out. It was highly unusual and unexpected in Russia. Especially for February. Viktor's parents—and several other unfortunate frozen-sculpture lovers—were crushed under blocks of melting ice. This is why he weeps so much."

Minister Szymanowicz nodded. "He once told a reporter, 'I weep as the ice wept—right before it killed my mama and my papa.'"

"That is so sad," said Beck.

"Totally," added Tommy. "What a bummer."

We all started sniffling a little. Our eyes were getting watery, like ice cubes in a tray that's been sitting on a kitchen counter too long.

Except Storm. She seldom gets emotional or teary-eyed about anything.

"So," she said loudly (so we could hear her over all the sobbing), "are we ready to hit the road here or what?"

"You honestly think you will find all of this stolen art at the North Pole?" asked Minister Szymanowicz.

"Given the clues fed to us by the E-Ones," said Mom, shooting me another look, "it remains our best guess. And if we're wrong? We won't quit searching until we retrieve your treasures—no matter where the quest may take us."

"And we'll find all that stuff stolen from those other museums too," said Tommy. "We're very good at tracking down things everybody else thinks are lost forever."

"Like our dad," I added. "After a couple false starts."

"Very well," said Minister Szymanowicz. "My

associates will put together everything you need for your expedition north. No expense shall be spared."

"*Spasibo,*" said Mom.

"You're welcome. These arrangements will, of course, take a little time." He opened up a filing cabinet, pulled out five small shopping bags featuring his ministry's snazzy official seal, and gave one to each of us. "Please, Kidd Family Treasure Hunters, accept these goodie bags with our compliments."

I checked mine out immediately. There was all sorts of fantastic free stuff inside: one of those matryoshka nesting dolls, a big slab of gingerbread, Alyonka chocolate bars, a Russian fur hat, a USB thumb drive, a three-pronged phone charger, and dried apricots (yuck).

"We have booked for you and your tutor a block of rooms in the magnificent Ararat Park hotel," the minister continued. "Enjoy your evening in Moscow. I hope you find the time to do some shopping, for soon you will need very warm, very heavy winter clothes. Tomorrow, you leave for the North Pole!"

CHAPTER 26

The Ararat Park Hyatt was an amazing hotel, maybe five minutes from the Kremlin, Red Square, and Saint Basil's Cathedral.

It was also pretty close to Moscow's extremely famous Bolshoi Theater, which would've been even more exciting if any of us (besides Mom) liked ballet. We grew up on a ship. Nobody wears tights and leaps around like that unless he's Peter Pan being attacked by pirates.

"We have your three rooms," said the uniformed guy behind the front desk.

"We only need two," said Mom.

"But Minister Szymanowicz specifically reserved—"

"Two will do." Mom turned to face Larissa Bukova. "You're fired."

"Excuse me?" said Larissa.

"Your tour-guide and tutorial services are no longer required. You are terminated. *Vy uvolyonnye s raboty*—dismissed from employment. No more talking, just get walking!"

Mom didn't explain her actions because (a) moms don't really need to do that and (b) Russian eyes and ears were everywhere!

When we got to our rooms, Mom put a finger to her lips.

Something was definitely up.

Mom gestured toward our goodie bags with the Ministry of Disasters and Bad Stuff emblem stickered to them.

I KNEW IT! THOSE DRIED APRICOTS WILL KILL YOU!

Without saying a single word, Mom ripped the sticker off her goodie bag, went into the bathroom, tossed the paper wad into the toilet, and flushed. Then, she pulled the phone charger and USB thumb drive out of the bag. Those, she dumped in the trash bin. She nodded and gestured to us to indicate that we should all do the same.

So we did.

After the final flush, Mom finally broke her silence.

"The goodie bags were bugged," she told us. "There was a very thin, miniature microphone hidden inside the ministry's official seal. The phone chargers and thumb drives were meant to tap into our e-mails, text messages and phone calls. The Russians executed a similar goodie bag espionage ploy during the G-Twenty summit held in Saint Petersburg back in 2013."

"They're spies!" said Beck.

"Yes," said Mom. "But, then again, so were your father and I."

"What about the rest of the goodies?" I asked, eyeing the chocolate.

Mom shook her head. "Sorry, Bick. They could have laced the food with something to make us sick. You can keep the hat and the dolls, though."

Great.

Tommy raised his hand. "Um, why'd you fire Larissa?"

"She is also a spy. Probably for the Russian police. Maybe Minister Szymanowicz."

"That's most likely why he called her 'Larachka,'" said Storm, who, don't forget, remembers every word anybody ever says. "Use of her nickname indicates that Minister Szymanowicz and Larissa have known each other for a long time."

I was right! I had a hunch those two were pals!

"Wait a second," said Tommy. "Are you sure? Because I think she really dug me."

"I'm sorry, Tommy," said Mom. "You can't trust anything she says or does."

The doorbell rang.

As our muscle, Tommy opened it. A very pretty room service waitress was standing in the hall, holding a silver platter covered by a dome.

"*Zdravstvuyte*," she said.

"Well, *zdravstvuyte* to you, too," said Tommy, giving the waitress the flirty look he practices in the bathroom mirror every morning. "What's your name?" he asked.

"Inna."

"Riiiight. Inna. That must be Russian for 'Angel.'"

We were all rolling our eyes.

The waitress? She just laughed and handed Tommy the tray.

"Enjoy your time in Moscow," she said, and then she turned on her heel and sashayed away.

"If you're here, don't worry—I will!"

The waitress just laughed again and kept on walking.

"Tommy?" said Mom, indicating with hand signals that Tommy should bring the tray into the room and close the door.

"And lock it," said Storm.

"Why?" I asked.

"Because," said Beck, "nobody ordered room service."

She was right.

So what was underneath that shiny silver dome?

CHAPTER 27

Mom raised the lid and discovered—you guessed it—another envelope with a wax E-1 seal.

"I'm going to send this clue to your father." Mom tapped the message into her high-tech watch.

Then she showed it to us.

STILL CAN'T FIND OUR SECRET TREASURE TROVE?

HERE'S ANOTHER HINT:

It is home to a strange race where only the strongest will make it to the finish line.

CHAPTER 28

"We're still talking North Pole!" insisted Storm.

"No way," I said.

"Way," said Storm. She seemed much happier since Mom fired Larissa. "The Arctic Circle is home to what has been billed as 'the coolest marathon in the world'—the North Pole Marathon."

"Seriously?" said Beck. "Who'd want to run twenty-six point two miles in the freezing cold?"

"Marathoners who can reach their personal best only when being chased by hungry polar bears," said Tommy.

"Last year," said Storm, "forty-five runners from twenty-two different countries participated. They helicoptered up to an international North Pole camp, dashed across the floating Arctic ice shelf, and enjoyed subzero temperatures averaging minus twenty-two degrees Fahrenheit. The entry fee for the event is approximately fifteen thousand dollars. However, you do get a free T-shirt."

"What's the winner get?" asked Beck. "A frozen icicle wreath to wear on her head?"

"Chya," said Tommy, who sounded like he was seriously considering signing up. "Plus bragging rights for a whole year."

"You guys?" I said. "You are seriously jumping to conclusions. There are all sorts of weird races in the world."

"Maybe," said Storm. "But we have to put this third clue together with the first two."

"The North Pole fits all three," added Beck.

"So might someplace else," I muttered, because nobody was really listening to me.

"We need to go shopping," said Mom.

"Running clothes?" asked Tommy. "For the marathon?"

"No. Thermal underwear. Parkas. Ski pants and goggles. Pack those furry Russian hats. I also want each and every one of us to be carrying a compact, high-definition video camera of some sort. We need to record everything we see on our journey north."

"So we can show everybody exactly how we didn't find the treasure?" I said sarcastically.

"Bick?" said Mom. "I know you have doubts but I need you to put those aside. We are going to the North Pole. We have serious work to do and priceless treasures to save! I suspect we might discover a real disaster when we reach the Arctic…"

Beck gasped. "You mean all the stolen artwork might've frozen into sheets of ice that somebody dropped and that Rembrandt shattered into a million tiny pieces?"

Mom didn't answer but she had that mysterious look on her face again. It's the one she gets whenever she's trying to hide a secret.

Yep. That's life with a CIA mom.

So we all went shopping.

While we hunted for winter clothes (always hard to do in the middle of the summer) and miniature video equipment, Beck and I discussed the situation. We were certain that Mom had some other reason for heading up to the North Pole.

"Maybe," I said to Beck as we tried on mukluks, "if you want to save the whole world, like Mom and Dad do, the best place to start is at the top."

"Or maybe," said Beck, "Mom and Dad just don't believe in any kind of summer vacation."

"Right. There's that."

Once our furry shopping spree was finished, we booked a flight from Moscow to Helsinki, Finland, with the assistance of Minister Szymanowicz. Once in Helsinki, we flew to Murmansk, a seaport located in the extreme northwest corner of Russia. From there, we set sail for the North Pole via the Barents Sea.

Studying the map, I figured we were in for a very frigid summer. On the bright side, maybe we'd get to meet a few narwhals.

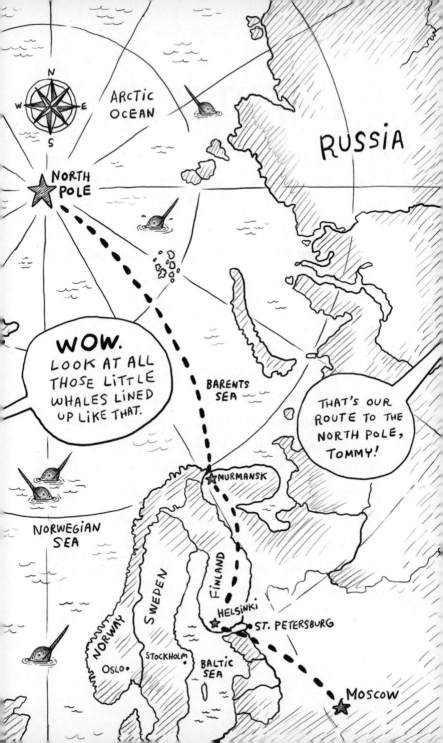

CHAPTER 29

We boarded the *Fifty Years of Victory*, the world's largest icebreaker, in Murmansk. It was nuclear-powered, so that meant it could churn through ice like a supersonic snow-cone machine. The ginormous ice cruncher had a spoon-shaped bow that was capable of breaking through frozen stuff nine feet thick! It also had its own helipad and helicopter, which meant it was capable of being totally awesome.

The captain informed us that it would take six days to reach what he called "ninety degrees north." That's nautical talk for the North Pole.

We all shot a ton of high-def of the journey. I knew the Arctic was going to be amazing, but seeing everything in person was mind-blowing. When we passed our first glaciers and the ship started cutting through the Arctic ice pack, it was really cool (pun courtesy of Storm).

During the voyage (think *Moby-Dick* with floating ice cubes), even though we felt as if we were in the middle of frozen nowhere, we weren't alone. We passed a few Russian oil tankers heading south as we churned our way north.

151

"Is there really oil up this far?" I asked. "Wouldn't it all be frozen?"

"Actually," said Storm, "the Arctic is believed to hold one-third of the world's remaining untapped oil and natural-gas resources. That's why the Russians built the Prirazlomnoye offshore drilling platform above the Arctic Circle. It's only six hundred and twenty miles from Murmansk."

"The Russians are extremely proud of their Arctic oil exports," said Mom. "And they will defend them at all costs. President Putin signed a law that allows oil and gas corporations to establish private armed security forces to defend their tankers and offshore oil rigs from any and all 'terrorists'—including environmental protesters from Greenpeace."

That would explain why those Zolin oil tankers we'd passed all had armies of security guards toting submachine guns patrolling their decks.

Finally, when we were all warm and cozy inside Mom's cabin (which she'd swept for listening devices), she told us why going to the North Pole was so super-important—even if we didn't find the Enlightened Ones' secret treasure trove.

"Our goal has never been to simply find sunken treasure, stolen artwork, and chests filled with gold and precious jewels," said Mom.

"That's true," said Tommy. "We also like to meet interesting people. Like that room-service waitress."

"Meeting fascinating and friendly people is fine, Tommy. But your father and I have always been interested in another kind of treasure, one

153

that's more valuable than any other because it's completely irreplaceable: the Earth. That's why we donate so much of the money we raise from our treasure hunting to environmental charities that help save the planet."

I put two and two together. "Is the North Pole in trouble?" I asked. "Is that the real reason we're going there?"

Mom nodded.

"Because of the Russians?"

"Not just them, Bick. Every country in the world wants the buried treasure that lies hidden beneath the polar ice cap."

"What buried treasure?" I blurted out.

"Well, here's a hint. It's nicknamed 'black gold,'" said Mom.

Oh yeah. Oil!

"And the more oil people pump out and burn," Mom explained, "the more damage they do, not just to the Arctic but to the whole global climate."

Wow.

When she put it like that, saving the Arctic was way more important than saving a Rembrandt.

Even Beck would have to agree with that.

"But what can one person or family do to save the planet?" asked Storm.

"Well, for starters," said Mom, "we can make sure we're not the only ones doing it! We need to spread the word."

She flicked on her video camera.

"Come on. Let's go hit the deck and get back to work!"

PART 2

THE TREASURE SAVERS

CHAPTER 30

We all bundled up, grabbed our video gear, and headed out to record everything we saw on our way to the North Pole.

No, we didn't see Santa Claus. Or Rudolph. Or even penguins. (Beck says that's because penguins are found only in Antarctica and the South Pole, but you probably knew that already.)

By the way, now that Mom had confirmed that our real reason for sailing to the North Pole wasn't to find the looted Russian art or the Enlightened Ones' secret art-treasure storage facility, I understood why Dad had to split. He, like me, knew the North Pole wasn't the real answer to the Enlightened Ones' clues. It was just too easy. But he and Mom needed an official, state-approved way to travel north and document what was happening to the Arctic environment without having those armies of oil-company security guards shooting their machine guns at us. In the meantime, Dad was free to hunt down the stolen goods.

I had to hand it to Mom and Dad. They knew what they were doing, even when it didn't seem like it!

Anyway, back aboard the *Fifty Years of Victory*, we spent three pretty awesome days crushing through the Arctic ice pack. We also shot some more amazingly beautiful video.

Beck and I saw polar bears and walruses. Storm memorized the songs of the seabirds soaring overhead. Sometimes, the blue glacier ice sang to us too! Unfortunately, the songs came from the glacier cracking and sloughing off sheets of ice, which made whining noises as they slid into the sea. Mom said it was evidence of global warming.

"There are no trees anywhere," said Tommy, stating the obvious. But actually, it was pretty incredible to look out and see nothing but flat ice islands, big and small, in all directions.

Except some of the snowdrifts were glowing flamingo pink!

"It's algae that grows only on snow," explained Storm. "A phenomenon due, in part, to all the guillemot guano."

"What's that?" I asked.

"Bird poop."

"And there goes some human waste," said Mom with a sigh. "The nonbiodegradable kind. A lot of what's wrong with the environment ends up here, guys. Trash and debris dumped into the oceans of the world get carried north-ward on underwater currents."

She zoomed in her camera on a lake of bobbing plastic that, to say the least, hadn't been properly recycled! We saw bottles, bags, and even tossed-out tub toys. Beck and I shot footage of it too.

"The amount of plastic debris and litter on the Arctic Ocean's seafloor has doubled in the past ten years," said Mom. "A lot is trapped in glaciers."

"Which," said Storm, "are melting at a record rate and unleashing a plastic avalanche."

We passed a glacier that looked like a box of ice cream somebody forgot to pop in the freezer. After a little ice singing, chunks slid down the side and, with a thunderous splash, belly-flopped into the sea.

"This is the real treasure we need to save, guys," said Mom as another wall of ice collapsed. "We need to record everything we see. Put it all together in a documentary."

"Don't worry, Mom, we're getting some really killer footage," I said.

"Maybe, if people get to see what's really happening at the North Pole—ice melting, animals in danger, the balance of nature being radically disturbed, the Russians threatening to come in and mess everything up with oil spills—"

Mom did not get to finish that thought.

Three burly men in bright yellow parkas surrounded us on the ship's bow. They looked extremely shady.

"Excuse me," said one in a thick Russian accent. "Why do you take pictures of that? It is just ice."

"The North Pole," said another one, pointing forward, "is, how do you Americans say, *north*."

All three of the scary men chuckled. Their foggy breath smelled like fish. Fish that had been smoking cigars.

I checked out the embroidered patch stitched to the arm of each of the three yellow parkas.

It resembled a *3* because it was the Russian letter for *Z*—just like we'd seen on that passing oil tanker.

Because our deck mates worked for the teenage billionaire Viktor Zolin!

CHAPTER 31

"You work for Viktor Zolin?" I said.

"*Da.* But now, we are here on what you call summer vacation. Forget Mexico or the Bahamas. We like to take cruises to more frigid climates."

More snickers from the three thugs. Their parkas were so poofy they might've been hiding weapons under their coats. Heck, they were so poofy they might've been hiding walruses.

"Well," said Beck, who really isn't afraid of anything or anybody, "we're only on this tub because your boss, the teenage billionaire, recommended us for this mission."

"What mission do you mean?" said one of the Russians. "Taking home movies of glaciers?" He held out his hand to Mom. "Give me the camera. Now."

"Excuse me?" said Mom.

"Viktor Zolin owns that glacier. He does not like people taking pictures of his property."

This time, Mom just laughed.

"You're joking, right?"

The Russian shook his head. "No joke. Putin sold it to him."

Mom rolled her eyes. "I'm sorry, what's your name?"

"Nikita. My name is Nikita."

"I'm sorry, Nikita, but Vladimir Putin does not own the Arctic Circle."

"Oh, really? Try telling him that!"

Mom was starting to lose her patience with Nikita. "Look, sir, many countries have laid claim to the Arctic Circle, not just Russia—Canada,

Norway, Denmark, and the United States."

Storm took over with the details. "Each country is allowed to explore potential oil reserves within two hundred miles of its coastline."

"Ah," said Nikita, "but several years ago, we Russians very cleverly sent a mini-submarine to the floor of the Arctic Ocean and planted our country's flag underwater. So the ocean is all ours!"

"Ha!" said Storm. "The United Nations tossed that claim out years ago."

"It does not matter. You may not take photographs of that iceberg without the express written consent of Viktor Zolin. Give me your camera, Mrs. Kidd, or you will force me to take it."

Mom did as she was commanded.

Probably because she realized the goons weren't packing walruses under their parkas.

Plus, Mom knew the four of us had snapped the same photographs and videos on our smartphones—the ones that were now cleverly hidden deep inside the pockets of our four parkas.

"You've got Mom's camera," said Tommy, "now back off, Nikita. We're the good guys, remember? We came all this way to find the four famous paintings stolen from your art museum in Saint Petersburg."

"You funny!" howled Nikita.

"No," I said. "That's an entirely different book series starring Jamie Grimm. He funny. We Kidds. We treasure hunters."

"We're not just treasure hunters," said Mom. "We're also people who are extremely worried about what's happening to the Arctic environment."

The three Russians stopped laughing.

Nikita reached inside his pocket. I heard a click.

Oh yeah. He was definitely packing.

CHAPTER 32

"What do you mean, you are worried about the environment?" said Nikita, puffing out his already puffy chest.

"This fragile ecosystem could easily be destroyed," said Mom. "By people like Viktor Zolin."

Yep. She went there. (I think Mom's the one Beck got her tough stuff from.)

"The Russian oil industry spills more than thirty million barrels on land each year," added Storm, who'd been spending time in her cabin memorizing Greenpeace web postings. "That's seven times the amount that leaked into the Gulf of Mexico during BP's *Deepwater Horizon* disaster."

"This is ice," said Nikita with a sinister smile. "This is not land."

"True," said Mom. "But over eighteen months, you guys spew four million barrels of oil into the Arctic Ocean."

Nikita narrowed his eyes. "Accidents happen this far north, Mrs. Kidd. To oil. To pipes. To *people*. Noses can freeze and snap off. Especially when these noses are being poked into matters they have no business investigating. We would not want to see this happen to you. Or your children."

"Whoa," said Tommy, bristling. "Is that a threat, dudes?"

"No. Just a friendly word of advice. As you cook the porridge, so you must eat it."

"Huh?" said Beck. "Who's cooking porridge?"

"I didn't see it on the breakfast buffet," I added.

"It is a Russian proverb!" shouted Nikita, looking like a big, angry bear.

The exasperated Russians shook their heads. "Do not say we did not warn you, Kidd Family Treasure Hunters! Many accidents happen on the ice every year. You do not wish to be one of them!"

Then they stomped away.

"Keep shooting footage, you guys," said Mom when she was sure they were gone. "We need to document all of this, the beauty of it all and what's at risk if we don't change some bad habits soon! Just don't let Zolin's goons catch you with your cameras up."

"There's only three of them," said Beck. "There are five of us shooting pictures."

"Four," said Mom. "They took my camera."

"No problem," said Tommy. "I have a couple spares in my cabin. I have to take a lot of selfies and text a lot to keep up with my many, you know, *friends*."

He wiggled his eyebrows.

We all kept taking pictures and recording footage for our Kidd family Arctic documentary— but never in a group. And never if we saw one of the Zolin heavies lurking nearby.

And then, finally, we reached the North Pole.

The icebreaker creaked and crunched to a stop. The grown-ups all popped open bottles of bubbly stuff and celebrated with a toast. Beck and I split a root beer.

We rushed off the boat with everybody else.

After posing for a few quick pics and Beck's family sketch, we heard a strange announcement: "Everyone, please join hands. It is time to dance around the world!"

CHAPTER 33

O kay, I have to admit—standing at the top of the world is incredibly awesome. Every direction we looked in was, basically, south.

We held hands with all the other passengers (including a South African girl whom Tommy fell in love with instantly) and did what the cruise director called "Our Special International Round Dance."

We'd never learned dancing on board the *Lost* but fortunately this dance was just walking in a circle around the North Pole, or 90 degrees north, as everybody's GPS app referred to it.

"Now," said the cruise director when we'd completed one rotation, "you have all literally walked around the world!"

"Awesome," Tommy shouted.

"But we're still going to sail around it," Beck said to Mom. "Right?"

"You promised," I added.

Mom nodded. "And save as many of this earth's treasures as we can."

176

Our cruise package included a backyard barbecue on the ice, a hot-air-balloon ride over the pole, and, for the totally adventurous (or totally insane), a plunge into the Arctic Ocean! Which one of us was dumb enough to do it? You guessed it. I think Tommy did it only because the girl from South Africa put on her bathing suit first.

We spotted Nikita and his Zolin Oil crew patrolling the ice pack with their weapons out.

Beck and Storm marched right up to the guys. Mom, Tommy (shivering in his wet swimsuit under his parka), and I followed close behind.

"What do you think you're doing with those rifles?" demanded Storm.

"Protecting you from polar bears," said the head goon, Nikita. "And, perhaps, yourselves."

"You will not shoot a polar bear!" said Beck.

"Polar bears are listed as a threatened species under the U.S. Endangered Species Act of 2008," said Storm, giving the Russians her total eco-tour-guide treatment. "Thanks to the ongoing loss of their sea-ice habitat due to global warming."

"Do you like polar bears, Kidd Family Treasure Hunters?" asked Nikita slyly.

"We're Americans," said Tommy. "We love every cute and cuddly critter on earth and/or YouTube!"

"The only way we'd want to shoot one," said Mom, "is with our cameras. But since you took mine, I can't do that either!"

"Do not despair," said the Russian. "You are in luck. There is a polar bear very near to where we now stand. See the paw prints? Change into your warm clothes, shivering boy in bathing suit. We will let you borrow our snowmobiles so you may track it."

"Excuse me?" said Mom.

Nikita shrugged. "Viktor Zolin called us on the ship's radiotelephone. He said we are to be nice to you since you are, indeed, doing this treasure-hunting favor for him. Who knows? Perhaps this polar bear is the one who stole the paintings from the Hermitage Museum."

His friends chuckled at his terrible joke.

"Are you mocking us?" asked Storm.

"No. We're joking. We funny, like this Jamie Grimm you told us about," said Nikita. He clapped his hands. "Quickly, change into your expedition gear. We will get the snowmobiles ready. You don't have much time before the ship turns around and heads back to Murmansk!"

CHAPTER 34

We all raced back to our cabins to put on our warmest expedition gear.

I wasn't so sure this was a smart idea (the same way I wasn't sure that the North Pole was the answer to the Enlightened Ones' clues).

"Um, Mom?" I said as we climbed up the decks to our cabins. "A couple hours ago, Viktor Zolin's flunkies were sort of threatening us. Now they want to loan us their snowmobiles? Don't you think that smells kind of fishy?"

"Nah," said Tommy. "That's the salmon from the barbecue. Wasn't it awesome? Amahle liked it too."

"I'm serious, you guys," I said. "Something's

not right about this. I don't trust those Zolin Oil guys. They're too…oily!"

"You're right, it's a risk," said Mom. "But, Bick, never forget who we are."

Right. We are the Kidds. The Wild Things. We live for action, adventure, and doing risky stuff like diving into freezing-cold water or borrowing skeevy henchmen's snowmobiles.

"Besides," said Mom, "if we have a chance of seeing a polar bear up close and personal in its native habitat, well, that's something I don't want you guys to miss. It'll remind us all why protecting the Arctic Circle is so important."

But then she told us to grab our go bags, just in case.

Whenever we're on an expedition, we all keep our most essential gear in small gym bags—our go bags—so we can grab them if we need to make a fast exit or escape. For me, that's clean socks (after our adventures in Africa, you know why clean, dry socks are always super-important), some spare clothes, and my baseball cap. Oh, and the most important thing for me is my journal, to record our treasure-hunting escapades. For Beck, it's her sketchbook. For Tommy? Duh, hair gel. And Storm always makes sure to tuck a few Hostess Twinkies into her go bag.

So even though we are like the Wild Things in that book by Maurice Sendak, we are also semi–Boy Scoutish too. We are always prepared. Like Dad says, "Hope for the best, prepare for the worst."

WHY DON'T TWINKIES EVER GO STALE??

Once we were all squared away with our subzero expedition gear and go bags, we headed back down to the ice.

"Enjoy," said Nikita and his thug buddies, who stood next to five snowmobiles. "We have checked your gas tanks. All is as it should be. Have much fun. Take many selfies with polar bears to post on Instagram. We shall see you when you return to the ship!"

We zoomed off across the frozen tundra. Fortunately, the trail of polar-bear prints was straight and clear.

We zipped along following the prints, and in no time at all, I couldn't even see the ginormous icebreaker boat behind us when I checked over my shoulder. I was starting to worry we wouldn't be able to find our way back, that our tracks would get buried by the blowing snow we were stirring up as we raced across the ice.

After about thirty minutes, the paw-print trail came to an end. But instead of the big white bear we were expecting, we came upon a cluster of men dressed in combat camo. Some were armed with guns and grenades.

And the reason the paw prints were so clear? One of the men was wearing paw-shaped snowshoes!

And he was holding a bazooka.

CHAPTER 35

"**B**ack to the boat!" shouted Mom.

She fishtailed her snowmobile hard to the right.

The four of us cut skidding arcs close behind her, our runners stuttering over frozen speed bumps in the ice.

"*Stoy!*" shouted one of the Russians. "Stop!"

Tommy cut a doughnut, spewing up a whirlwind of frosty white ice in his wake, so he could whip out his binoculars and see what we were up against.

"They're Russian Airborne!" he shouted. "Elite paratroopers! They have skis and they know how to use them!"

"Good thing we have snowmobiles!" I hollered at Tommy, circling back to make sure he didn't spend too much time gawking at our Russian pursuers. "Come on! We can outrun 'em!"

Tommy and I popped snow wheelies and sped across the rutted ice. We were forced to swerve away from our ship when bullets started popping into the ice near us.

"Gun it!" I heard Beck shout up ahead.

Mom, Storm, and Beck sent their snowmobiles sailing in the air like they were leaping horses.

Bringing up the rear, Tommy and I soon found out why.

The sleek white landscape we were jetting across was basically an ice island. We were running out of frozen tundra fast.

Tommy and I would need to make the leap too.

We twisted our throttles to gun our engines while squeezing hard on the brakes.

"Now!" shouted Tommy right before we hit the jagged edge of the ice floe.

We let go of the brake handles and took off!

We made it across.

Mom, Beck, and Storm were waiting on the other side, engines idling.

"No way are those guys making that leap on skis!" said Tommy.

"They don't have a ramp!" I added.

"I snapped a shot of you two flying between ice floes," said Beck.

"We looked totally awesome, right?"

"Sure," said Storm. "But the real reason for the photograph was to document the breaking up of the Arctic ice pack due to climate change. Animal lives are at risk."

"Um, so are ours," I said, because I could see that pack of speed-skiing Russian paratroopers schussing after us in hot pursuit.

"Let's rock and roll," said Mom. She revved her engine.

It sort of sputtered.

Then mine started knocking and pinging.

Tommy's just wheezed and conked out. Beck's belched a black cloud of exhaust. Storm's shivered like it was suddenly cold.

Then all five snowmobiles died.

"Nikita!" Beck and I shouted at the same time. (It's a twin thing.)

I punched a gloved fist into my gloved palm. "This is what he meant when he said they'd checked our gas tanks and all was 'as it should be'!"

"They wanted us to run out of fuel," said Beck, "so we'd all die of exposure after an unfortunate and mysterious snowmobile incident."

"How ironic," said Storm, who's big on gallows humor. "Our dying wish will be for a few more gallons of gasoline, which, of course, can be obtained only by pumping oil out of the earth."

"You guys?" said Tommy. "Maybe we should all put up our arms like we're surrendering. And if anyone has a white flag, now would be a good time to start waving it."

"Why?" demanded Beck.

"Because," said Tommy, "those Russian paratrooper dudes are Navy SEAL good. They just ski-jumped the water gap without a ramp and they're headed right for us. With guns!"

189

CHAPTER 36

We all did as Tommy suggested and threw up our arms.

"Don't shoot!" I shouted at the Russian soldiers skiing straight at us across the ice. "We surrender-ski!"

Storm rolled her eyes. I guess just adding *ski* to the end of a word doesn't make it Russian, even when the Russians you are talking to are on skis.

"Ne strelyayte!" shouted Storm. *"My Kiddsy!"*

"We know who you are, Kidd Family Treasure Hunters," said the squad leader as the Russian paratroopers skied right up to us.

The squad leader, who was wearing a white ski mask that made him look like a wrestler from the WWE (or a jack-o'-lantern snowman), crunched slowly across the pack ice to Mom.

"I am Colonel Dragunov, here to tell you that Minister Szymanowicz is not pleased," he said menacingly through the mouth hole of his mask. "He sent you here to the North Pole to find stolen art masterpieces, not to take a joyride across the ice."

"And why did he send you?" asked Mom, who, don't forget, used to be a spy and didn't threaten easily. "We only just arrived at the pole a few hours ago. We were out here on a scouting expedition. Getting the lay of the land. Looking for any unexpected storage structures."

"That's right," I said. "The art thieves might've built themselves a frozen Fortress of Solitude out here somewhere. You ever heard of cold storage? Well, that's what this would be. A subzero warehouse, filled with all sorts of treasures. Rembrandts, Picassos, those other guys..."

Dragunov squinted at me like I was an annoying narwhal. "Is this true?" he asked Mom. "Were you searching for this fortress of ice?"

"It is one possibility we are considering," said Mom. "Definitely."

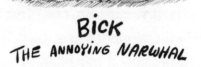

BiCK
THE ANNOYING NARWHAL

"Here is something else for you to consider." He reached into his chest pocket.

I flinched because I was half expecting him to pull out one of those gnarly survival knives with a sawtooth blade on top.

Instead, the Russian pulled out an envelope sealed with wax.

Another clue from the Enlightened Ones!

I noticed a small hole in the top of it as he handed it to Mom.

"This was found nailed to a wall of the Hermitage Museum in the blank spot where our revered Rembrandt used to hang. Minister Szymanowicz gave us the order to fly north and parachute over the North Pole to deliver it to you. Apparently, it is a very important document, *da*?"

"It could very well be," said Mom.

She tore open the envelope.

"Is it a ransom note from the art thieves?" asked Colonel Dragunov.

Mom shook her head. "No. It's another clue."

"A clue about what?"

"Where your country's lost treasures might be stored, along with priceless art objects and antiquities stolen from collections all around the globe!"

Dragunov leaned in close to Mom. He was twice her size. But you know what? Mom had had so much martial arts training, I think she could've taken the guy.

"Use this clue," said the soldier. "Find our art. Do it fast. Because my boots are thin and my feet are cold!"

LOOKING FOR
OUR STOLEN TREASURES?

HERE'S SOMETHING
YOU SHOULD KNOW:

*It's always 103 above
even when you're 35 below.*

After checking out this fourth clue, I was positive about one thing.

We were freezing our butts off in the totally wrong spot.

CHAPTER 37

Mom studied the new clue.

She passed it to Tommy, who passed it to Storm, who passed it to Beck and me.

"One hundred and three above?" mumbled Beck so the paratrooper couldn't hear. "That sounds like the temperature of that mosquito-riddled African jungle we nearly died in!"

"But it didn't go down to thirty-five below, ever!" I mumbled back. "Not even at night when we were so cold we were shivering."

"So?" said Dragunov. "Have you solved the riddle and discovered where you will find our missing masterpieces?"

Mom smiled. "Colonel, it's not that simple.

This is only one clue of many that we need to analyze, consider, and—"

The colonel tugged off his ski mask so we could see how mad he was.

"Find our treasure now! No more talking. You twirl your tongue like the cow twirls its tail!"

"I beg your pardon?"

"It's another Russian saying, Mom," Storm informed her.

"Well, it's not a very pleasant one."

Six soldiers knelt in the snow. They weren't praying. They were aiming their rifles at us!

"You will follow the clues and take us to the secret treasure-hiding place right now," threatened the colonel, "or else!"

Mom grinned. Propped her hands on her hips.

"Or else what?" she asked. (See, I told you she didn't threaten easily.) "What are you going to do, Colonel? Order your men to shoot us? With the whole world watching?"

"*Pah*. The world is not watching."

"Yes, it is." She gestured toward the crisp blue sky. "There's a CIA drone overhead right now. It's recording every move we make. And every one *you* make too."

"I do not believe this. Why would the CIA send a drone to watch over you?"

"It's part of the benefits package," I said, since I'm the best at spinning stories and making junk up. "When you retire from the CIA, which Mom just did, you can sign up for their drone-protection plan."

"You are like your mother, little boy," snarled the Russian. "You lie with every word."

"Did you just call my twin brother a liar?" asked Beck angrily.

"He did," I said. "But first he called me a little boy!"

"That's even worse."

"I know. Makes me a little liar!"

"And we're both the same height!"

"So you insulted my sister too!"

Yep. The two of us were in total Twin Tirade mode, but this one didn't get a number because we weren't directing it at each other. This one was just for the Russian bullies in the white snowsuits. Our faces were so hot, we melted every snowflake that dared to come within an inch of our skin.

"Enough!" shouted the colonel. "Silence! Rope is good when it is long; speech is good when it is short!"

"Did you memorize a Russian proverb book on the flight up or what?" snapped Beck.

"Zamolchite! Zatknite!"

"Oh, they'll shut up," said Mom, who knew enough Russian to translate that one. "The second you quit hassling us!"

Mom was totally backing us up as we faced off against the elite Russian menace. It was so cool. In a totally life-threatening sort of way.

"Your youngest children are very cute and clever, Mrs. Kidd," said the colonel. "But in Russia, we do not care for cute *or* clever. So we will shoot them. Then we will shoot you and the other two. Then we will bury you and your four children under the ice."

"Whoa," said Tommy. "Sounds like you've blocked out a pretty busy afternoon, dude. Did you guys bring shovels and ice picks? For the burying part, I mean."

Before Dragunov could threaten to throw our bodies to the sharks instead, a *chirp-chirp* sound rang out cheerfully.

The colonel held his hand out while glaring at us. One of his soldiers gave him a sleek black communications device with a stubby antenna: a satellite phone!

"Da? Ochen' khorosho, gospodin. Ya zdelayu, kak vy skazali. Ya by predpochitayu, chtoby postrelyat' ikh vsekh. Khorosho. Ya ne eto zdelayu. Khoroshevo dnya."

"What'd he say?" Mom asked Storm.

"That he'll do what the caller told him to do even though he'd rather shoot us all. Then he told the caller to have a nice day."

The colonel tossed the satellite phone back to his radioman.

"So," he finally said to Mom, looking disappointed that his superiors wouldn't let him shoot us. "Do you have a plan as to where you will search next?"

Just then, several dogsleds appeared on the horizon.

"Of course," said Mom. "In fact, here come our rides now."

CHAPTER 38

Three sleds, each pulled by a team of panting huskies, glided across the ice toward us.

Every sled carried a driver wrapped in fur. As the sleds drew nearer, I noticed that the drivers were Eskimos, who, as I learned from Storm, I should actually call Inuit.

"Well, hello!" Tommy called out to the dogsled in the middle. "Thanks for dropping by. You're the answer to all our prayers. Especially mine."

Tommy wasn't just saying this because the Inuit dogsleds had shown up in the nick of time. Judging by his frostbite-risking hair-smoothing, he'd already fallen in love at first sight with the pretty Inuk girl driving the middle sled.

"These are our local contacts," Mom said to the Russian colonel, who was scratching his head in confusion. "They've discovered a few leads that might help us in our investigation. Please tell Minister Szymanowicz that we will contact him the instant we know more about the location of your stolen art."

"You will contact him?" asked the Russian. "How?"

Mom held out her hand. "You will give me your satellite telephone."

"That is unacceptable," said the Russian. "We will accompany you and your so-called local contacts until you find the paintings."

"Great," I said, "you guys can be in charge of scooping the dog poop."

"What?"

"Those sled dogs don't run on oil," said Beck. "They run on meat. They eat, they poop, they run, they poop. Get it, poop-head?"

"You children are disgusting!" said the Russian, scrunching up his face like he just smelled a bad batch of carbonated bread juice. (Seriously. That's a thing in Russia. They call it *kvass*.)

"You think we're disgusting now?" I said. "Wait till you spend some quality time with us."

"Bick seldom bathes," added Beck.

"Well, not when it's freezing out."

"You didn't bathe in the tropics either!"

"Because when I am exploring the earth, I enjoy smelling earthy!"

"The earth doesn't reek as bad as you!"

"Says who?"

"Me and half the people in China. They built that Great Wall to keep you and your stench out!"

Yep. We were really whaling on each other, big-time—battling like the most obnoxious brats in the world. When we're in full-blown Twin Tirade mode, there's not a grown-up on the planet who wants to spend more than ten seconds anywhere near us.

"Quick!" shouted the colonel. "Summon the helicopters. Initiate the extraction package."

The radioman made a fast call on the satellite phone.

"Give me that!" said the colonel, grabbing the phone from his radio operator. He tossed it to Mom. "Call Minister Szymanowicz when you find the paintings. We are out of here!"

The Russians scrambled into the helicopter and took off.

"Works every time," said Beck.

"Mission accomplished," I replied, giving Beck a high five.

Mom went up to the eldest of the Inuit.

"We seek help," she said.

"Tatiksarpok," translated Storm.

Yep. She speaks Inuit too. Memorized it on the boat ride north "just in case." I told you we Kidds are always prepared!

The old man in the fur parka motioned toward his sled. "Please. Join us."

"Whoa," said Tommy. He gestured toward the pretty girl. "Does she speak English too?"

The old man smiled. "Fortunately for you, no!"

Laughing, we climbed into the dogsleds and took off!

And you know what?

Sled dogs poop on the run. Constantly.

CHAPTER 39

Our new friends took us to where they had erected a temporary shelter.

An igloo!

"Our village is farther south," explained the elder once we were all snug inside the cozy dome of ice blocks. "But my good friend, your husband, Thomas Kidd, requested that we come north to keep an eye on 'the most valuable treasures in the world.' His family."

"Whoa," I said. "You know our dad?"

The elder nodded. "Many years ago, when he was taking cold-weather survival training in Greenland for his work at the Agency, I was his instructor. One day, I clumsily slipped and fell through a fishing hole in the ice. Your father dove in after me. Fortunately, he is a very excellent diver. He can hold his breath for a very long time."

"We all know how to do that," said Beck. "Holding your breath for a really long time is a skill you need to hunt treasure on shipwrecks. And when you live with Bick, the human stink bomb."

The elder laughed. "Be that as it may, I owe my life to your father. So when he called, we came right away."

"Thanks," said Tommy, who was winking at the pretty girl. "You know, you're such a hottie, I'm surprised the walls aren't melting."

"Forgive my son," said Mom. "He falls in love at least twice a day."

"Nuh-uh," said Tommy. "This is for reals."

The girl smiled at Tommy. Beck and I rolled our eyes at each other.

"Her name is Nagojut," said the elder. "She is my granddaughter."

"Her name is beautiful—just like the rest of her," said Tommy. "What does Nagojut mean?"

"'Friendly one.'"

"Ohhh," said Tommy. "I like the sound of that!"

Since we were all starving, we chowed down on *akutaq* and bannock. That's berries mixed with blubber smeared on top of flatbread. Kind of the PB and J of the North Pole. It was pretty good, in an "I'm so hungry I'll eat anything no matter how disgusting it looks, smells, or tastes" kind of way.

After we ate, the elder, whose name we learned was Sata Adjuk, explained a little bit about how the Inuit build an igloo, or snow hut.

"We cut the blocks of snow by hand with a knife. The warmth inside mixed with the cold wind outside will cement the snow blocks together firmly. The air pockets in the snow act like insulation…"

While he told us all this, I noticed that Mom kept fidgeting with the Russian satellite telephone.

"You okay, Mom?" asked Tommy, because he saw it too.

She gave us a weak grin. "Just worried about your father. At least I have you guys and our new Inuit friends. He's all alone, wherever he is."

"He'll be fine," I said, even though I was starting to worry too.

"I'm not so sure about that, Bick," said Storm. "If we're on the wrong trail to find the stolen art, then Dad might be on the right one. He could be close to finding the Enlightened Ones' secret hiding spot. If so, he's probably in danger, big-time."

Storm. She always says whatever's on her mind, even when you sort of wish she wouldn't.

"Your father has many friends," said Sata, "in many corners of the world. If he is facing danger, he will not need to face it alone."

"You're right," said Mom. "But I wish I could

share this new clue with him. He needs it more than we do."

"So text it to him," said Tommy.

"There're no cell towers this far north, hon," said Mom. "We're too far from the ship for Wi-Fi. And I don't think this igloo is wired for the Internet."

"So?" I said. "Use the satellite phone."

Mom hesitated. "The Russians will, most likely, intercept the message and read it."

"That's okay," said Beck. "They're the ones who gave us the fourth clue. They want Dad working on finding their stolen art as much as we do."

Mom nodded.

She powered up the satellite phone. The status indicator glowed green. She thumbed in a quick note to Dad:

No longer actively searching for missing Russian masterpieces at the North Pole. Check out the fourth clue, received at Hermitage Museum.

She attached a photo of the clue and hit send.

"Now," she said, "let's just hope your father is someplace where it's one hundred and three above even when you're thirty-five below!"

Yep. Whatever that means.

CHAPTER 40

We spent the night in the igloo.

Sata, Nagojut, and their Inuit traveling companion, Bob, built themselves another ice hut (in like thirty minutes) so us Kidds could spread out inside our very own frozen dome.

Exhausted, I fell asleep fast but had the worst nightmare ever!

I dreamed that the icebreaker turned around and sailed back to Murmansk without us. Viktor Zolin's oily minions told everybody that we'd slipped on the ice and fallen down a fishing hole.

"And there was nobody around who could hold his breath long enough to save them," said Nikita, who looked even scarier in my dream.

I was tossing and turning when I heard a
very loud, piercing beep that wouldn't quit. In
my dream, I thought it was an alarm for the
nuclear reactor on my nightmare's nuclear-
powered icebreaker, which was about to go,
well, nuclear and have a meltdown.

Terrified, I woke up with a jolt.

And bumped my head on the igloo roof, which
was basically a giant ice cube.

Everybody else in the igloo was also sitting up, wondering who set an alarm for so early in the morning.

It was the satellite phone. A red light was flashing on it.

Someone was calling.

Mom looked to Storm. Nodded.

Storm pushed the answer button. *"Da?"* she said. *"Alyo?"*

And then she listened and said *"Da"* a few more times. Finally, she said, *"Spasibo za etu informatsiyu. Do svidaniya,"* and hit the off button.

I HOPE YOU HAVE A **GOOD** REASON FOR CALLING AT THIS HOUR!

"Who was that?" asked Mom.

"An undercover Russian military operative stationed on board the *Fifty Years of Victory* checking in with our departed paratrooper friends. He reports that our cruise ship has left the North Pole and that representatives of Zolin Oil told the crew that we had elected to stay at

217

the pole so we could photograph walruses and polar bears."

So my nightmare had actually come true. The icebreaker was headed back to Russia without us.

We were stranded at the top of the world.

Mom and Tommy went next door and quickly roused our new Inuit friends in their igloo.

"An interesting development," said Sata, sounding surprisingly mellow, considering the news. Then again, being stuck in the Arctic Circle was no big deal for him. This was his home, after all!

"It's a bummer, for sure," said Tommy, making goo-goo eyes at Nagojut. "But on the plus side, I wouldn't mind spending more time familiarizing myself with your local customs. For instance, dating. How does that work? Do you guys really rub noses instead of kissing? If so, can someone show me how it's done? Maybe Nagojut?"

Mom cleared her throat.

Tommy knocked it off.

"Gather up your gear," said Sata. "We will dogsled to the Barneo drifting-ice research station. It is like a small settlement with housing for explorers and special buildings for all kinds of scientific equipment. They will have communications gear as well."

"Wait a second," said Storm. "Isn't the Barneo drifting-ice station run by the Russians?"

"Yes," said Sata.

"We definitely can't go there," I blurted out. "They're the bad guys!"

"Not all Russians are bad, Bick," said Mom. "The Russians at the research station will be explorers and scientists. Just like us!"

Tommy raised his hand. "Will your granddaughter be coming with us?" he asked.

"Of course," said Sata. "She is the best dogsledder in all of the Arctic."

"Then what are we waiting for, guys?" said Tommy. "Let's hit the road!"

"There are no roads," said Storm. "Just ice."

"Whatever. Come on. We're heading back to ninety degrees north to see if Nagojut and I can make it even hotter!"

CHAPTER 41

We climbed aboard the three dogsleds and, once again, slipped, slid, and bounced across the frozen tundra.

As you know, we Kidds have been on some pretty awesome thrill rides in our adventures. But I don't think any of them can compare to soaring across the ice behind a pack of happily yapping dogs while breathing in the crisp, clean Arctic air. (Except, you know, when one of the dogs had to do its business; then the air got a little polluted.)

"When we come to a turn," said Bob, our driver,

"lean into it or we will all be eating snow. You will see."

So Beck and I leaned into every turn, and Bob did the same, standing up behind us with one foot hovering over the ice-brake bar.

The other two dogsleds were ahead of us. But suddenly, I heard dogs barking—behind us!

I whipped around.

We were being chased! By two guys on dogsleds. They were dressed in speckled white Arctic camo, just like the elite Airborne soldiers we'd met the day before.

The Russians' sleds were extremely high-tech. They had sleek aluminum frames with way better aerodynamic design than our humble Inuit rides.

Bob, our driver, shouted, "Mush! Hike!" at the dogs.

Then he shouted at us!

"Hang on, Kidds. We will move very, very fast now. You will see." He started making kissing noises.

Our dogs picked up speed. Soon, they were galloping.

221

So were the dogs in front of the other two sleds in our pack.

But the Russians yelled the same kind of stuff at their dogs and started cracking their whips.

They were gaining on us.

"Ice floe on the right!" shouted Mom. "Water!"

Great. We were skirting the edge of another floating ice island.

The swifter Russians moved so they were parallel with us on the left. Then they started angling in. They were trying to force us into the Arctic Ocean.

Suddenly, up ahead, Nagojut shouted, "Come! Haw!"

Her dog team executed an unbelievable 180-degree hairpin turn to the left and went racing straight at the two Russian sleds.

The Russian drivers stomped down hard on their brakes.

Their sleek sledges skidded to a halt so fast, the lead lines went slack. Their dogs ended up in a loose clump and started snarling. In a flash, they were on one another, yelping, snapping, and wrestling in a ferocious canine cage match.

"Never let your towline go slack when dogsledding," said Bob. "If you do, your dogs will attack one another. You will see."

"Um, I think we just did," said Beck.

We took off. Before long, the two Russian sleds and their snarling dogs became distant dots on the horizon.

I kind of hoped the dogs would stop fighting and go after the drivers.

Meanwhile, our way to the research station had just gotten totally clear!

CHAPTER 42

Hours later, we arrived safely at Barneo.

The research station was amazing, especially after we'd spent the previous night in an igloo sleeping on hardpack snow. There were heated tents, a mess hall and kitchen, modules for storing scientific gear, and bio-toilets. All on a drifting ice floe that moved with the currents. There was also an airstrip—a floating runway for cargo planes to land on.

And because the floating ice is so thin, it eventually melts away, and the whole thing— the camp and the runway—has to be rebuilt every year!

North Pole drifting stations do all sorts of important stuff while they float around the Arctic Sea like slowly melting Popsicles. Scientists at Barneo monitor the ice pack, the temperature, the sea depth, the currents, the weather, and even the marine life. Best of all, this research station also had free Wi-Fi!

"They weren't soldiers," said Mom, tapping her watch, which was back online. "My sources tell me

226

that Viktor Zolin sent out another two-man team of goons to track us. He ordered them to wear Russian military camo to scare us into thinking they were here on official business. Apparently, the teenage billionaire learned through intercepts of Russian military communications that we had survived our snowmobile adventure."

"Why is Zolin after us?" I asked.

"Maybe he doesn't want our documentary to ever make it to the web."

"Why not?" said Beck. "Does he own the North Pole too? Did President Putin sell that to him also?"

Mom just shook her head. "I sure hope not."

Later, we met up with some very cool explorers and researchers. Some, of course, were Russians and they were very nice. Very brainy too.

"Zolin Oil is extremely sloppy and accident-prone," said Dr. Dimitry Zagorean over a mug of cocoa in the mess hall. "A disgrace to the Russian nation. Not too long ago, they were using lasers to cut through the ice and they sliced a pump pipe. The oil spill was contained quickly, but, trust me, it won't be the last accident. Zolin cuts corners the same way they cut their own pipes!"

A researcher, a toxicologist named Dr. Andrew Pardue who had a very bushy beard with clumps of chunky peanut butter stuck in it, told us horror stories about the floating plastic we'd seen earlier.

"Sadly, I have discovered toxins I had never seen before in bears and reindeer," said Dr. Pardue. "They are coming from the nonbiodegradable plastic being dumped into the oceans. Worse are the microbeads—tiny plastic particles found in shower gels, face scrubs, and smile-whitening toothpastes."

Tommy got defensive. "Why's everybody looking at me?"

"Ten million tons of plastic are dumped into rivers, lakes, and seas every year," said another scientist, Dr. Casie Bowman. "Much of it drifts north and ends up in the bellies of polar bears."

"So the bears are, like, eating face scrubs and toothpaste?" said Tommy.

"No, hon," said Mom. "They're probably just eating fish who ate the plastic that floated up from America."

"And, of course," said Dr. Bowman, "although many politicians and business tycoons will deny it, the polar ice cap is melting at an alarming rate. When ice melts, it turns into water. When water goes into the ocean, the sea level rises. When the sea level rises, the coastlines change."

"So," joked Dr. Pardue, "if you don't own beach-front property, don't worry. Pretty soon you will!"

After getting settled in our tents, Beck and I strolled outside to see what the sun looks like at midnight because, during the summer at the North Pole, it never really sets; it just sort of bounces off the horizon.

In the distance, we saw the two guys in camo we thought we'd lost during the crazy dogsled chase.

They were just standing there, not budging and not caring that it was a brisk 25 degrees out.

Either that or they were frozen stiff.

"You guys?" Mom called from her tent. "We just heard from Dad. The Enlightened Ones sent him another clue!"

AS YOU PROBABLY KNOW, YOUR FAMILY IS SEARCHING IN THE WRONG PLACE.

SO HERE'S ANOTHER CLUE, JUST FOR YOU:

One night, there were 160 endangered species outside. The next morning, they were gone.

CHAPTER 43

Okay, that last clue was just loopy.

A hundred and sixty endangered species wiped out in a single night? Where could that happen? It made absolutely no sense at all to me.

"We never really thought the Enlightened Ones had hidden their treasure trove here," confided Mom when we huddled for a family meeting the next morning.

That's what I've been saying!

"Then shouldn't we be helping Dad find it?" Tommy asked.

"There are important things we can do while we're up here," said Mom. "This is a once-in-a-lifetime opportunity to help save the true treasures of the earth. Everybody, grab your cameras. Interview the scientists. Shoot lots of footage. We need to document the truth of what's happening in the Arctic Circle and share it with the world!"

"Um," I said, "can we eat breakfast first?"

"Please?" said Beck. "They have real food here. And none of it is from the blubber food group."

"Fine," said Mom. "We eat. Then we go shoot more video!"

We left our tent (happy to see that Viktor Zolin's two frozen goons in fake camo were no longer spying on us) and hit the busy mess hall. The food wasn't fantastic, but, like Beck said, it sure tasted better than blubber berries on dry Inuit toast. I grabbed a few slices of cold cuts, sausage, and bacon and stuffed them in my pockets to snack on later.

"Maybe we should split up," said Tommy after

breakfast. "We can grab more footage that way. We can have three teams—Beck and Bick, Storm and Mom, me and Nagojut."

"Nagojut went home, Tommy," said Storm.

"Fine. Then it'll just be me and my memories." He sighed and looked heartbroken until a very attractive Norwegian scientist strolled past our table, carrying a tray. "Unless, of course, *she's* available for some fieldwork. Excuse me, guys. Catch you later."

Tommy chased after the Norse goddess.

The rest of us bundled up and headed outdoors.

"Storm and I will go east," said Mom. "You guys go west. But, and this is super-important, don't go too far!"

"Mom?" said Beck. "We know how to take care of ourselves."

"It's true," I added. "Because you guys taught us how to do it!"

We split up. Beck and I hiked west and shot some pretty awesome stuff for our Kidd family film.

We saw polar bears (and tried to warn them about the plasticky-tasting fish). We also photographed walruses, musk oxen, caribou (also known as reindeer), and an arctic fox!

You can see the best of the best on our supercool website: treasurehuntersbooks.com.

"This is so awesome!" exclaimed Beck.

"Yep," I said, "it can't get much better than this."

I was right. But it could get worse.

Because the next time I aimed my camera, guess what I saw.

A wolf!

CHAPTER 44

"Did it see you?" asked Beck as the wolf stared straight into my lens.

"I think so. I mean, it sure saw my camera!"

"When encountering a wolf," said Beck, reciting some memorized survival guide, "you don't want the wolf to see you."

"Too late."

"Okay. Where there's one wolf, there's usually two or three more."

I swung my camera left, then right. "Four. I count four."

"Quit looking at them!"

"How else can I count them?"

Beck dropped her eyes and started backing

up. "Back away slowly, Bick. Avoid eye contact. Wolves see eye contact as a challenge."

"Who would want to challenge a wolf?" I said, staring down at my feet as I shuffled backward.

"Other wolves."

"Don't they know the no-eye-contact rule?"

"Bick?"

"Yeah?"

"Shut up."

I tried that. For maybe ten seconds.

"Should we run?" I asked.

"No. Wolves run faster."

"Just keep them in front of you, Bick," coached Beck. "If we show them our backs, their predatory instincts will kick in."

"And by *predatory*, you mean 'surviving by eating others,' correct?"

"Yes, Bick."

"Just checking."

"This really isn't the best time for a vocab drill, bro."

"Oh, I don't know. If we're going to die, I'd like to die a little smarter."

Beck and I moved back two steps. The wolves prowled forward two paces.

"If only we had some meat," said Beck, "we could probably distract them and get away."

"Like bacon, salami, and sausages?"

"Exactly. That would be a miracle."

I patted my bulging (and somewhat smelly) pocket. "Actually, I've got some."

"What?"

"From breakfast. I thought I might want a snack later on—"

"Throw it, Bick!" Beck muttered as the wolves

began circling us. "As hard and as far as you can."

"Well...then what are we going to do for a snack?"

One of the wolves closed in.

Beck eyed it nervously. "Toss it or I'll throw *you* to the wolves!"

"What? You wouldn't really—"

"Throw it! Now!" she screamed.

I stuffed my hand into my parka pocket and squished all the slimy bacon, salami, and sausages together into one ginormous meatball.

Then I reared back and hurled it as far as I could.

The four wolves took off.

The sound of their scrabbling paws churning through the snow and ice scared a caribou behind a drift. It bolted out and hightailed it across the icy plain.

The swiftest wolf fielded my meatball and gobbled it down in one gulp. Then he and his three buddies took off after the fleeing reindeer. I was sort of hoping it was one of Santa's so it could lift off the ground and fly to safety.

"Come on," said Beck. "*Now* we run!"

We tore across the ice as fast as we could, heading for the research station.

I saw something glinting in the sun.

"Wait! Hold up."

Beck and I went over to inspect the object. It was an empty steel cage. I sniffed the inside…it smelled like wet dogs. Or, more likely, wet wolves.

"Someone shipped these wolves up here!" I said.

"No wonder Zolin's two goons disappeared. They decided to let the wolves do their dirty work."

Beck saw something and used her boot to

scrape away some icy snow from the base of the cage.

"It looks like some sort of shipping tag," she said, dropping to her knees to dig through the snow with her mittens. She showed me the tag.

It had a big Russian 3 printed on it.

Except it wasn't a *3*.

It was a *Z*.

"Zolin!" I said.

Beck nodded. "Guess this explains why his dogs are wolfhounds!"

CHAPTER 45

B eck and I made it back to the drifting research station without running into any more wolves.

We were safe! So were Mom, Tommy, and Storm.

Mom and Tommy were pretty impressed with our daring wolf escape. Storm was more impressed with Beck's memorization skills.

The five of us regrouped in our family tent and shared our photos and videos.

I hadn't snapped any shots of the wolves. For one thing, they weren't really local animals. For another, my fingers had been frozen. With fear.

"Great work, guys," said Mom as she flipped through all the pix. "We'll do some editing and upload—"

Just then, our tent door flew open and not because of a blast of freezing Arctic wind. It was kicked open by a group of Russian soldiers led by (hold on to your earflapped fur hat) that blabbermouth of a tutor and tour guide, Larissa Bukova!

I knew she was in cahoots with Minister Szymanowicz! She's a walking, talking natural disaster.

"You are to leave here immediately," said Larissa. She sounded way angrier than I remembered. Even when we were in prison she didn't sound this annoyed.

Mom tried to speak.

Larissa held up her hand to stop her.

"We know that you are—how did the fifth clue put it? Ah, yes, 'searching in the wrong place.'"

"Whoa," said Tommy. "You read that message from Dad?"

"*Da.*"

"But that was private and confidential!"

"So?"

Tommy looked very disappointed in his Russian crush. "That's…that's…*spying.*"

"*Da.* Something your mother and father are quite familiar with. We also, of course, picked up your earlier satellite-phone text communication with Professor Thomas Kidd. The message where you confess that you are, and I quote, 'no longer actively searching for missing Russian masterpieces at the North Pole.'"

"The most recent clues from the Enlightened Ones suggest we are looking in the wrong spot," explained Mom.

"Of course they do!" snapped Larissa. "You, your husband, and your children have been playing us for fools. Creating this Enlightened Ones conspiracy-theory nonsense. Leading us on what you Americans call a wild-goose chase so your husband can abscond with our historic treasures!"

"That's not true!"

"Pack up your things. We are taking you back to Russia! Minister Szymanowicz and Inspector Gorky would like to speak with you. You are never, ever to return to the North Pole. Ever!"

So we were basically given ten seconds to grab our go bags. Then we were marched across the ice to that floating airport, where a Russian cargo plane was waiting with its engines running.

CHAPTER 46

I t was a pretty long flight back to Mother Russia. Pretty bumpy too. Riding in the cargo hold of a transport plane isn't exactly the same as flying first class.

"The trip to the pole wasn't a waste, kids," said Mom. "We have our videos and photos."

"We can cut them together to make an awesome documentary," said Storm. "The guys at Greenpeace might be able to help us too."

Mom nodded. "For the next few days, we can shift back into treasure-hunter mode and focus on finding the missing Russian masterpieces stolen from the Hermitage."

"Won't they just be in storage with all the other Enlightened Ones' loot?" I asked.

"Not necessarily, Bick. The two things may not even be connected. So, while Dad searches for the E-Ones' treasure trove, we'll focus on finding the four stolen paintings from Saint Petersburg. Let's hope Minister Szymanowicz or Inspector Gorky has some fresh ideas and leads."

"They do," said Storm sarcastically. "They think Dad did it."

"We're really going to help the Russians?" grumbled Beck. "They're our enemies."

I nodded. "They basically banned us from the North Pole. For life!"

"They've been spying on us all along!" added Storm. "Tapping our phones. Intercepting our e-mails and texts."

"Plus"—Tommy sighed—"one of them broke my heart."

"They're pure evil," I said. "So why would we want to help these no-goodniks find their stolen treasure?"

Mom fixed us all with a very stern look.

It got pretty quiet in the hold of that transport plane. Well, as quiet as a droning Antonov AN-74 ever gets.

"The Russians aren't our enemies," Mom said in her super-calm voice, which is actually scarier than her angry one. "There are no bad people, no bad nations. Not the Russians. Not the North Koreans. It's always just a small group of knuckleheads in a country. Usually rich greedy men. Not always. But usually."

I wish some of those rich greedy men had heard Mom say that in her super-calm voice.

If they had, they'd know the Kidd Family Treasure Hunters were coming to get 'em!

CHAPTER 47

We finally landed at Pulkovo International Airport, just south of Saint Petersburg.

The Saint Petersburg in Russia wasn't as warm and sunny as the Saint Petersburg in Florida, but after all the ice, igloos, and glaciers, we were totally pumped to be south of the Arctic Circle again.

Our armed escorts ushered us through the cool, modern terminal.

Straight to Inspector Gorky.

"Welcome back, treasure hunters," said

Inspector Gorky with a fake smile. "Did you happen to find the motherland's four missing masterpieces in an ice-sculpture garden protected by mutant polar bears?"

Given his major 'tude, maybe Inspector Gorky should change his name to Inspector Snarky.

"We were wrong about the North Pole," admitted Mom.

"No!" said Inspector Gorky with heavy sarcasm. "What a surprise. And where is your husband, the renowned art historian and treasure hunter Professor Thomas Kidd?"

"We're not sure," I said.

"He's on his own secret mission," added Beck.

"And where might that be?" asked the Russian detective. "Somewhere in New York or London, where he's talking to shady art dealers who would love to sell our national treasures to the highest bidder?"

"Inspector," said Storm brusquely, because that's how she says everything, "for the last time, Dad did not steal Leonardo da Vinci's *Madonna Litta,* Caravaggio's *The Lute Player,* Giorgione's *Judith,* or Rembrandt's *Danaë*!"

"Really?" said Inspector Gorky. "Then why have you memorized the artists and titles of the four paintings still missing from the Hermitage Museum?"

"I have a photographic memory. It's what I do. I memorize stuff."

STORM'S PHOTOGRAPHIC MEMORY AT WORK!

"Dr. Kidd has been on another continent, tracking down the Enlightened Ones' secret treasure trove," explained Mom. "We have reason to believe it is nowhere near Russia. We also now suspect that they were not the ones who stole the art out of the Hermitage."

"Oh, really?" said the inspector. "And why do you think this?"

"Because, while we were in flight, my husband texted me."

Gorky arched an eyebrow. "You had Wi-Fi in the rear end of a cargo plane?"

"No," said Beck. "We had satellites. Mom and Dad used to work for the CIA, remember?"

"You can see it on this," said Mom, unstrapping her high-tech wristwatch.

Inspector Gorky put on his reading glasses, squinted, and scrolled through the block of text on the watch screen, which was about the size of a postage stamp. We all held our breath while we waited for him to finish.

Finally, he looked up and nodded. At least the fake smile was gone.

"*Otlichno.* Very good. Reading this, I am convinced that the Enlightened Ones are not our thieves. Neither is your husband. In fact, I now suspect someone here in Russia is our culprit. Therefore, since one who sits between two chairs may easily fall down, that is where we must focus our investigation."

"Huh?" said Tommy.

"Another Russian proverb," said Storm. "It means if you keep trying to follow two paths, you'll end up going nowhere."

"*Da.* I have decided to follow only one. Yours. Find our treasures, Kidd Family Treasure Hunters. Find them soon!"

With that, he handed Mom back her watch.

And the sixth clue!

CHAPTER 48

All Beck and I could figure out was that maybe the Enlightened Ones' secret hiding place was somewhere in America because D.C. could be Washington, D.C. Then again, it could be some other D.C.—maybe direct current, which, according to our walking Wikipedia, Storm, is electricity traveling in one direction (not to be confused with the boy band One Direction), like you get from batteries or solar cells. So that might mean the bad-guy billionaires were stashing their stolen art in a battery factory. Or a solar farm.

Or maybe D.C. means that D.C. Comics is somehow involved. They're the guys who gave us Batman, Superman, Wonder Woman and all sorts of evil villains.

As you can tell, all we had were guesses about D.C.

Same with H.H. We have absolutely no idea who or what those letters stand for. Mom suggested Horatio Hornblower. Probably because he was a sailor in a book, just like us.

Basically, we were getting nowhere, fast.

"Let's focus on the part of the message about the missing Russian masterpieces," said Beck. "We need to start somewhere."

"Good idea," I said. "It says:

According to the E-1s (and you have to figure billionaires like that have spies and paid inform- ants everywhere), our art thief was a Russian local. Maybe even an "art hater" right here in Saint Petersburg.

"How can anyone hate art?" wondered Beck, our family artiste, as Inspector Gorky ferried us from the airport to our hotel.

"Maybe Picasso turned them into a cube or something," suggested Tommy. "Or maybe they don't like all those paintings and statues of peo- ple not wearing any clothes." He paused. "You're right, Beck. How can anyone hate art?"

Inspector Gorky dropped us off at the State Hermitage Museum Official Hotel. "Get some rest," he advised. "Thaw out from your time at the North Pole. Tomorrow, your most important treasure hunt begins. Find the four missing masterpieces. There will be trouble if the cobbler starts making pies."

We all just nodded. I figured it was another one of Inspector Gorky's famous Russian sayings that I wouldn't be saying to anybody anytime soon.

We picked up our keys at the front desk and went upstairs to our rooms.

Which weren't exactly empty.

Someone was waiting for us.

And it wasn't room service with a platter of Russian caviar.

It was despicable Uncle Timothy!

CHAPTER 49

"I hope you kids don't mind," said Uncle Timothy as we just stood there gawking at him, "but I ate all the cheese straws in the minibar. All the M&M's and Famous Amos cookies too. Breaking out of the most secure federal penitentiary in America really makes you work up an appetite."

He touched his ear.

"Roger that," he said to whoever was on the other end of his communication. "The lambs are in the pen. I'll run the canary trap. Set up the dead drop and organize an OP for the OPO."

"Timothy?" said Mom.

"Hang on," he said to his earpiece. "Yes, Sue?"

"I was with the CIA, remember?"

"Affirmative."

"So I understand spy jargon."

Uncle T touched his ear again. "Let me get back to you. *Do svidaniya.*"

"What are you doing here, Timothy?" demanded Mom. "And why did you just tell your new boss that we're lambs and you're going to run a canary trap to expose an information leak?"

"Because this operation is so classified, we can't afford any leaks. Heck, I had to pretend to be a triple agent, get convicted of high treason, spend time in the Alcatraz of the Rockies, and make a daring escape through an extremely foul sewer pipe just to protect you and my four favorite little lambs!"

"Baaaah," said Storm. Not because she wanted to sound sheep-y, but because she didn't believe a word Uncle T was saying.

"I'm serious," said Uncle Timothy. "Everything has been leading up to this one single extremely crucial operation. Everything: The search for the Grecian urn. The trek through Africa. Your time

265

in China. The recovery of the art stolen by the Nazis. Every illegal art dealer that you—Tommy, Storm, Bickford, and Rebecca—have taken down so far, all the treasure you've recovered, it's all small potatoes compared to the big fish behind this Hermitage heist."

"You're mixing your metaphors," said Storm. "Potatoes don't swim in water."

Uncle Timothy probably gave Storm a dirty look. I couldn't tell for sure. His sunglasses were so mirrored I didn't know what his eyes were really doing behind all that shiny silver.

"Timothy," said Mom, "do you have a lead on who stole the art out of the Hermitage?"

"I might."

"Good. Because so far, we've got nothing."

Interesting. Mom didn't share the latest E-1 clue about the culprit being a local with Uncle T.

"All right, children," said Uncle Timothy, "kindly give us the room. Your mother and I need to talk. This is strictly an adults-only conversation. No children allowed."

"So," I said, "how come you get to stay, Uncle T?"

My sibs cracked up. Mom too. We were laughing so hard, we were holding our sides.

Uncle Timothy whipped off his sunglasses, a move he made only when he wanted to glare at you to show how serious he was.

"I'm serious," he said. (See? I told you.)

"Like a chess master, I've been running an extremely long game against the most cunning, clever, and crafty art thief in the world. He is the mastermind behind this recent rash of museum smash-and-grabs."

"Is it the Enlightened Ones?" I asked.

Uncle Timothy chuckled. "You read too many comic books, Bickford. The Enlightened Ones are a myth. They don't really exist."

"Then why did they send us so many clues about their stolen-art warehouse?" demanded Beck.

"Because the real culprits wanted your father out of Russia and out of the picture. But that was all part of my master plan too. With your father gone, the top dog would lower his guard. Giving your mother and me a very slim window of opportunity to swoop in and nab him."

Mom was furrowing her brow. She didn't trust Uncle Timothy any more than the rest of us. But I could tell she wanted to hear him out.

"Go to your rooms, guys," she said. "Uncle Timothy and I need to talk."

"In private!" added Uncle Timothy.

"Fine," said Tommy. "Just don't eat all the cashews too."

Uncle Timothy grinned. "Already have."

I just shook my head. Of course he had!

Because Uncle Timothy was a cashew-, cheese-straw-, and cookie-snitching creep!

CHAPTER 50

W e *did not* go to our rooms.

Hey, we're the Kidd kids. We live for action, adventure, and the adrenaline rush of finding something the whole world thinks is lost forever. Plus, not to brag, but when Mom and Dad were both out of the picture, the four of us did pretty well up against some fairly overwhelming odds and incredibly skeevy characters.

So we had our own powwow—with no adults— downstairs in the hotel's super-fancy tearoom.

"All that talk about minibar food made me hungry," said Tommy, eyeballing the spread of sweets, sausages, and smoked fish served alongside smoky-flavored black tea.

"I can't believe Mom is even talking with weird Uncle Timothy," said Beck.

"She kind of has to," I said. "He might still be working for the CIA on a top secret project."

"In a maximum-security prison cell?" said Tommy. "You'd think they'd give him a better office."

"Yeah," added Storm, "one without a concrete bed and pebble pillows."

271

"We should go find the stolen paintings ourselves," I said. "Like we found the Grecian urns and the paintings the Nazis looted in World War Two. We'd do a better job than Uncle Timothy, that's for sure."

"Fine," said Beck. "Where do you suggest we start looking?"

"Russia!" I said. "That's what the sixth clue said: the thief is a local!"

Beck narrowed her eyes and scowled at me. "Hello! That just means he or she is a Russian, Bickford."

I narrowed *my* eyes and scowled right back.

Yep. We were launching into Twin Tirade 608.

"If he's local," I insisted, "then he has to be in Russia."

"Not all Russians are in Russia at all times, Bickford," said Beck.

"Well, Rebecca," I replied, "there are more Russians in Russia than anywhere else."

"So?" said Beck. "That doesn't mean that the Russian we're looking for is in Russia."

"Maybe we should forget the Russian angle and concentrate on art haters," Beck continued tirading.

"Why?"

"Because there's only, like, two or three of them in the whole world!" said Beck.

"Are you kidding? Lots of people all over the world hate art!"

"Really?" said Beck, propping her hands on her hips. "Well, I'm not too crazy about them either."

"Me neither!" I screamed.

"I know that."

"I love your art!" I told her.

"Your writing's okay too," said Beck.

"Then why are we yelling at each other?"

"I forget."

"Me too."

"Want to go find an art-hating Russian?" asked Beck.

"Definitely. Let's start in Russia."

"Good idea."

And just like that, our tempest in a teapot (or tsunami in a samovar) was over.

When we'd completely cooled down and Tommy had finished his sixth salmon and cream cheese slider, Storm finally piped up.

"Let's go back to the scene of the crime," she suggested. "There might be a clue in the museum that we missed the first time through."

So the four of us hiked over to the Hermitage Museum. Just us kids, no grown-ups allowed. Like I said, we've done pretty well treasure hunting on our own without any adult supervision. Plus, children's admission at the art museum was probably way cheaper than what they charged adults.

Anyway, what was the worst that could happen?

CHAPTER 51

So out we went, around the block to the Hermitage art museum in Saint Petersburg, home of "mostly okay" Russian people, plus a few bad ones who make billions from oil sales and don't care if they have to melt the North Pole to do it.

We entered the museum and started to scatter.

Beck wanted to take a quick side trip to see the Dutch paintings on permanent display. "There might be more Rembrandts!"

Tommy wanted to see the Armorer's Art of the Middle East from the Fifteenth to Nineteenth Centuries.

"They have gnarly-looking swords," he said. "The kind with curved blades!"

I was sort of interested in the gift shop because they sold fake Fabergé eggs. Chocolate ones too.

"Anybody else still hungry?" I asked. "I need a quick candy break."

"Not me," said Tommy. "I ate all those little finger sandwiches, which, when you think about it, is kind of a gross name for food. I mean, who wants to eat a sandwich with a finger in it?"

"You know, Tommy, the gift shop might sell fake swords—"

"You guys?" said Storm, sounding extremely frustrated. "We need to focus. We're not here as tourists. We're here because we're treasure hunters!"

"Storm's right," said Tommy. "My bad."

"Our bad too," Beck and I said together.

Determined to find a clue we might've missed the first time, we marched past all sorts of incredible artworks and amazing ceiling decorations

to get to the gallery where the four masterpieces used to hang.

We entered the room where the thief had stolen the four paintings.

"They've been back!" Beck gasped when she saw what was hanging where the stolen art used to be. "The criminals have returned to the scene of the crime."

"What do you mean?" I asked, looking around for some suspicious Russian bad-guys.

"Look! Only an art hater could replace master-pieces by Leonardo da Vinci, Caravaggio, Giorgione, and Rembrandt with these modern mega-monstrosities!"

She was so upset, I thought her head might explode.

I looked closer at the new paintings that had been hung up and understood what she meant.

You see, the last time we visited this gallery, right after the theft, there were four blank spaces where the wallpaper was a little brighter than the rest of the wall because they'd been covered by picture frames for so many years.

Now those empty spots were filled with four of the most hideous paintings imaginable: a picture of a clown, a portrait of the late Elvis Presley (both painted on black velvet), a giant cat with big eyes, and a bunch of dogs playing a card game.

CHAPTER 52

"Who would dare put those horrible nightmares on the walls of one of the most respected art museums in the world?" Beck fumed.

"Maybe it's a new exhibit," I suggested. "Ugly American Art."

"I kind of like the cat," said Tommy. "He reminds me of that famous grumpy cat on YouTube."

"It's horrible," said Storm. "Beck is right— only an absolute art hater would hang these four eyesores in a museum as prestigious as the Hermitage."

"They're trying to get everybody to hate art as much as they do," said Beck, making urping noises like she might hurl. "And it just might work!"

"Over there," said Tommy. "That security-guard lady. She probably knows what's going on."

"Let's go find out," I said.

The four of us headed over to ask the security guard a few questions. She looked like she might've been the grumpier sister of that guard we'd bumped into at the Fabergé Museum when we first arrived in Saint Petersburg. I wondered if the cat in the painting was hers.

"Excuse me, madame," said Storm.

"Da?"

Storm never got to ask her question.

Because Tommy was tapping her on the shoulder.

Behind the museum guard were six big men, all of them wearing creepy rubber Vladimir Putin masks!

And it wasn't Halloween!

We turned on our heels and started walking fast.

The six frozen-faced Putins followed us.

We picked up our pace.

The Putins did the same thing.

"We need to go back and find out who hung up that horrible art," Beck said as she trotted ahead.

"Chya," said Tommy. "Definitely. But not right now."

With that, he started running.

The rest of us raced after him down a long hall lined with paintings. We dodged around a statue of a woman wrestling a wild boar (don't ask me why—there was no time to read the little explanation card) with the Putins still in hot pursuit.

We finally reached an unbelievably ornate set of steps—what Storm called the Jordan Staircase. It had steps going up both sides.

"Go left!" shouted Tommy.

So we did.

We came to a landing and I looked over my shoulder. "We lost them!"

"Excellent," said Tommy.

We rounded the landing and sprinted down the final set of red-carpeted stairs, taking them two at a time.

When we reached the bottom, guess who we ran into.

Yep. The six masked Putins.

Guess they went right when we went left.

CHAPTER 53

"**Y**ikes!"

They yelped first.

I think they were as startled to run into us as we were to run into them. Especially when we barreled into them at top speed.

Then a third party entered the picture.

The nasty security guard.

"There is no running in this museum!" she scolded us. "No rubber Halloween masks either. Behave yourselves or leave!"

Ashamed, the six Putins hung their heads. We did too.

"Do not make me come running after you again!"

"Since you're here," said Storm, "can I ask you an art-related question?"

"Nyet," said the guard. Then she stomped away.

As it turned out, that was probably for the best.

Three of the six Putins tugged off their rubber masks. Three did not. The man in the middle stepped forward.

"Uncle Timothy sent us," he whispered with what sure sounded like a Russian accent. "We work for the same...*company?*"

He gave us a big, knowing wink.

"The CIA, *da?*" said one of his comrades, also sounding extremely Russian.

Now you see why it was a good thing Storm didn't get her question answered by the art matron lady—if she had, the bad guys might've heard the answer too. We had no idea what "company" Uncle Timothy worked for these days. If it was the CIA, how come so many of their operatives had thick Russian accents? We could trust the men in the rubber masks about as much as we could trust Uncle Timothy—not at all.

"We don't want for you little ones to get hurt," said a third unmasked Russian.

"So is that why you chased us down a slippery marble staircase?" asked Beck.

"And almost caused us to smack into a statue?" I added. "Those things are made out of rock."

"I don't like running," said Storm. "Ever."

"Me neither," said Tommy. "It messes up my hair."

"Look, small children," said the head goon, "your uncle Teemothy is most worried. When he could not find you—"

"Hey," I said, "we've been lost in the jungles of

Africa, feared missing in China, and stranded in the middle of the ocean."

"I got lost in a mall once too," added Tommy.

"But we always end up fine," I said. "So tell Uncle Timothy, 'Thanks, but no thanks.'"

"And then," said Beck, "tell him good-bye."

"Do as the Kidd Family Treasure Hunters suggest," said a familiar voice.

It was Inspector Gorky, descending the grand staircase.

"You three?" he said to the men still wearing masks. "Have you come here to rob a bank?"

The men didn't speak but they shook their rubbery heads.

But they still didn't take off their masks.

"Good," said Inspector Gorky. "Then leave. And take your friends."

Surprisingly, Uncle Timothy's "coworkers" did exactly what the police detective told them to do.

Inspector Gorky turned to us. "So, Kidds, have you found our missing masterpieces?"

We all shook our heads.

"Well, then—have you found any clues?"

"Maybe," said Storm.

"But then those bad guys interrupted us," I added.

"It was like a totally major clue too!" said Tommy. "Serious bummer that the masked marauders busted in on us like that."

"So go," said Gorky. "Continue on your quest. Although you may not see me, I will have your back. But be careful—not everyone who wears a hood is a monk."

We all just nodded.

Then we dashed up the steps and headed down the art-filled corridors toward the gallery with the black-velvet portrait of Elvis and the sad clown.

Where we ran straight into Uncle Timothy.

And Mom!

CHAPTER 54

"Why did you guys take off?" asked Mom, a look of genuine concern on her face.

"We wanted to get a head start on the investigation," I said.

"Yeah," said Beck. "While you two were chatting, the trail was growing colder."

"All right," said Mom, giving us an annoyed look, "this foolishness has got to stop!"

"Um, what foolishness are you talking about specifically?" asked Tommy.

"Taking off without telling me where you're going. Running up and down the corridors of an esteemed art institution."

"Oh, *that* foolishness. Gotcha."

"From now on," Mom continued, "we only do foolish things *together*."

"Yeah," said Uncle Timothy. "As a family."

"Um, no, you're not part of this family," said Beck. "You're not our real uncle."

"Your father always called me Uncle Timothy—"

"You're not *his* uncle either."

"Come on, Mom," I said, jabbing a thumb toward Uncle T, "family? Seriously?"

"I am absolutely, positively serious about

every word I just said." She looked at all of us sternly. I had a feeling she was doing this to keep Uncle Timothy close and within our sights. It would be harder for him to double-cross us that way.

"O-kay," said Beck, rolling her eyes because Uncle Timothy was smiling so smugly. "Guess we better show the rest of our 'family' the huge clues we just discovered."

"What clues?" Uncle Timothy was extremely interested.

Storm stepped forward.

"We have reason to suspect that the thief who stole the four masterpieces from this museum has serious issues centered around art," she said because she'd memorized all of those psychology books by Sigmund Freud, Ivan Pavlov, and Dr. Phil. "He or, for the sake of argument, she is what psychiatrists would label an art hater."

Storm clasped her hands behind her back and started pacing. She was in full lecture mode.

"As Professor Gregory S. Parks of Wake Forest University in his critical analysis of 'Gettin' Jiggy wit It' points out, and I quote, 'No matter what they say, haters are not dispassionate and objective people when it comes to their hated object. In essence, they are emotionally motivated to hate.'"

Uncle Timothy peered over the tops of his sunglasses. "Huh?" he said.

"Haters aren't just gonna hate," said Tommy. "There's gonna be a reason for it."

"Correct," said Storm.

"You guys have completely lost me," said Mom.

"We think the sicko art-hating thief returned to the scene of the crime," said Beck, gesturing toward the adjoining gallery. "It wasn't enough for him to steal the four masterpieces. He had to replace that beautiful artwork with a collection of grotesque horrors."

"Come on," I said. "We'll show you."

We walked Mom and Uncle Timothy into the portrait gallery so they could see the cat-tastrophe (not to mention the Elvis, dog, and clown disasters) for themselves.

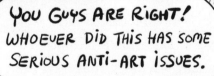
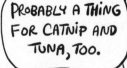

YOU GUYS ARE RIGHT! WHOEVER DID THIS HAS SOME SERIOUS ANTI-ART ISSUES.

PROBABLY A THING FOR CATNIP AND TUNA, TOO.

EXCUSE ME I THINK I'M GOING TO HOCK UP A HAIRBALL!

NOPE, NOT GOING TO LET YOU READ OR WRITE MY THOUGHTS. I'M FAR TOO GOOD A SPY FOR THAT!

CHAPTER 55

"We wanted to ask that security guard over there if she knew who donated the four repulsive paintings," said Beck. "But Uncle Timothy's six comrades with the rubber Putin pusses chased us out of the room before we had the chance."

"They didn't *chase* you," said Uncle Timothy. "They executed a flanking security maneuver known as the flying hex box to set up an impenetrable perimeter of protection."

"Nah," said Beck. "They chased us."

"And," I added, "three of them wouldn't take

off their masks. It was almost as if they were afraid to show their faces."

"Do they have bad zits?" Tommy asked Uncle Timothy. "Because, I remember when I broke out, I didn't want anybody to see me. I even covered up all the mirrors and shiny surfaces on our ship—"

"Stay here, you guys," said Mom. "I'll go talk to the nice lady."

Uncle Timothy touched his earpiece. "I've got a call to make."

"Um," said Tommy, "I thought we were supposed to do foolish stuff together from now on?"

Mom smiled. "You're right. Let's all go."

So all of us, including Uncle T, shuffled across the room in a bunch and surrounded the burly security guard.

"Excuse me, madame," said Mom, super-politely.

"Da?"

"Can you tell us, when were the cat, clown, dog, and Elvis paintings added to this gallery?"

"Recently."

"They don't really seem to fit with the other paintings on display."

The guard shrugged. "I do not understand art. I like to watch TV. Love *Masha and the Bear*. Is cute."

"I see," said Mom.

"But do you know who contributed these four new works to the museum?" asked Beck.

"*Da*. Anonymous. He donates many pieces. Paintings, statues, ancient artifacts. When Anonymous heard we had lost four paintings, he gave us four more." She shrugged again. "For me, a painting is a painting."

"But the substitute paintings are horrible!" shrieked Beck. "Why would the Hermitage, one of the greatest art museums in the whole world, agree to hang such ugly eyesores on its walls?"

The security guard grinned and rubbed two fingers back and forth across her thumb, giving us the universal sign for *Money! Money! Money!*

"Mr. Anonymous?" she said, checking to make sure no one was eavesdropping on our conversation. "He is very, very rich. One of our most eccentric and generous Russian billionaires. If he wants to donate pictures of Elvis, cats, dogs, and sad clowns, they will let him. They also say he does not really like art. In fact..." She looked around one more time to make absolutely certain her superiors couldn't hear. "I have heard that Anonymous hates art and hopes to one day see all of these other masterpieces disappear!"

As soon as she said that, a museum official came into the room. She abruptly left us and went back to standing by the doorway looking bored.

Sensing we wouldn't get any more information

from the guard, we left the museum and headed back to the hotel.

"So," said Mom when we were all gathered in the living room of her suite, "how do we find an art hater?"

"Easy for me," joked Uncle Timothy. "I just look in a mirror."

Beck glared at him.

"Sorry, Rebecca. I like action movies. Football. Drawing pictures and painting them in? That's for kindergartners."

After Uncle Timothy said that, Beck whipped out her sketchbook and drew this:

CHAPTER 56

We spent the next week camped out in the living room of Mom's hotel suite researching the art thefts around the world.

Don't forget, the Hermitage hadn't been the only museum hit by art thieves in the past several months. Priceless paintings were also stolen out of the Louvre in Paris, the Metropolitan Museum of Art in New York City, and the Saatchi Gallery in London.

We gathered all the information we could find, hoping to uncover some sort of link connecting all the heists.

We were at it 24/7—making connections, making mistakes, making our stomachs ache by eating horrible Russian pizza. Instead of four cheeses, our Russian pie had four fishes—sardines, tuna, mackerel, and salmon. To make it grosser, it was topped off with onions, herbs, and little red fish eggs.

Did I mention it's also served cold? Bleh.

On day seven, Mom sent Uncle Timothy away

on what she called a "ghost-surveillance" detail. Was Uncle T looking for ghosts? I mean, they would make pretty good spies. While he was out, we heard from Dad.

Guess what?

HE'D FOUND THE ENLIGHTENED ONES' SECRET TREASURE TROVE!

Woo-hoo!

We were all practically dancing for joy. Except Tommy. Dancing, like running, messes up his hair.

"I'll be rejoining you guys very soon," he said, never giving us a hint as to where he was or where he had discovered the stolen loot, like any good spy. "I am working with a team of art historians and appraisers, putting together a complete inventory of the masterpieces stashed in the Enlightened Ones' cleverly hidden warehouse."

"Did they have the four paintings stolen from the Hermitage?" asked Mom.

"No," said Dad. "But the Louvre, the Met, and the Saatchi Gallery are going to be extremely happy. The Enlightened Ones were the end buyers for their stolen masterpieces."

"So," said Mom, "we can focus our treasure hunting on Leonardo da Vinci's *Madonna Litta,* Caravaggio's *The Lute Player,* Giorgione's *Judith,* and Rembrandt's *Danaë*?"

"Exactly. Whoever stole the artwork in Saint Petersburg wasn't collaborating with the Enlightened Ones. He was, most likely, a lone wolf."

"And an art hater," added Beck.

"And," Dad added, "it'll be harder to find a thief

304

who's working solo, since he'll leave less of a trail."

"We've put together a preliminary psychological profile," said Storm.

"Good work," said Dad. "And the ghost?"

"Under control," reported Mom.

Seriously, what ghost?

"You guys are the best," Dad said.

We all told him how proud we were of him. Then he told us how proud he was of us.

When he hung up, I asked Mom what the ghost thing was about.

Timothy, she mouthed silently. "He's going to be helping us with our plans, even if he doesn't know it."

I wanted to ask more, but I knew better than to talk about it in our hotel room, which was sure to be bugged.

So we went back to work.

More cold pizza, bad sandwiches, and Tarhun soda, which, believe it or not, is a carbonated drink flavored with tarragon herbs. Yes, it's gross. Like drinking parsley.

Around noon on day eight of pinning stuff

on the walls, I was a little bored. Okay, I was a *lot* bored.

So was Beck. It's a twin thing.

"We're getting nowhere," said Beck with an exasperated sigh.

"And I can't eat any more of that fish pizza."

We both flopped down on the sofa and started flipping through hotel magazines while Mom, Storm, and Tommy kept pinning junk to the wall. (The hotel maids were going to hate us when we checked out.) My magazine was a glossy travel guide called *See Saint Petersburg!* It was all about nearby attractions and upcoming events.

And that's where I found the big clue!

The one that would (finally) lead us to the four missing masterpieces.

CHAPTER 57

It was an article (written in stilted English) called "Happy Winter-Wonderland Activities for the Whole Happy Family to Enjoy Happily."

Apparently, in February, when the weather got really cold, a team of "fourteen ice artists" would be building an ice palace in the center of Saint Petersburg. It would be modeled after the first one erected in the city in 1740 by Empress Anna Ivanovna to celebrate her tenth anniversary as ruler and Russia's victory in the Turkish war. There were pictures and everything.

That's when something our chatty tutor and tour guide, Larissa Bukova, had told us weeks ago came flooding back into my head.

Saint Petersburg had built one of these ice palaces before!

Ten years ago, to be exact.

And it turned out to be deadly for the teenage billionaire Viktor Zolin's parents.

It was a freak accident, Larissa had told us. The ice palace had crushed Viktor Zolin's parents when it melted during an unexpected February heat wave.

The palace that was, according to the magazine, also a "magnificent frozen work of art"!

"Of course!" I blurted out. "He hates art because art killed his mother and father!"

"Huh?" said Beck, who was flipping through a magazine that seemed to be all about shoes and purses. "Who hates art? I mean, besides Uncle Timothy?"

"Viktor Zolin!" I said. "I'll bet anything he's our guy. The art hater who stole those four paintings."

That got Mom's, Storm's, and Tommy's attention.

Fortunately, Uncle Timothy wasn't in the room. He had gone to the corner store to buy a meat pie and a bottle of glass cleaner for his mirrored shades.

"But Zolin is a major contributor to the Hermitage," said Mom.

"They even let him bring his wolfhounds into the gallery so they can poop on the floor," said Tommy.

"Inspector Gorky told us Zolin is 'one of our most eccentric and generous Russian billionaires,'" said Beck.

"Which," I reminded them, "is exactly how the security-guard lady described the anonymous donor of the four hideous pictures."

"If it was Zolin," said Storm, "it would be easy for him to 'generously' and 'anonymously' donate those paintings and get them hung in such a prestigious gallery."

"It's like you said, Storm!" I went on. "There has to be a reason for a hater to hate. Viktor Zolin hates art because art made him an orphan!"

Mom jumped up and gave me a hug. "It's the best lead we've got. Let's see where it takes us!"

CHAPTER 58

We rushed downstairs and squeezed into a taxicab.

We probably needed two cabs but Mom had said that we had to do our foolishness as a family from now on. So we all foolishly smooshed together in the backseat. It was like a rolling group hug. With arm cramps.

"So, um, where exactly are we going?" asked Tommy.

"Viktor Zolin's home!" said Mom. "Timothy can get us the location." Mom whipped out her satellite phone, poking Storm with its stubby antenna.

"Ow!"

"Sorry about that, hon," said Mom.

"No worries," said Storm.

Then Mom speed-dialed Uncle T and thumbed the speakerphone button.

"This is Red Rooster," answered Uncle Timothy from wherever he was (he wasn't really getting into the whole togetherness thing, which was fine by us). "Go ahead, Mama Bear. Is the porridge in the pot too hot?"

Mom rolled her eyes. Sometimes Uncle Tim's spy lingo was complete gibberish, so twisted that even former professional spies like her couldn't understand what the heck he was saying.

"Timothy," said Mom, dropping the whole barn-animal code-name stuff, "do you have any hard geographic intel on Viktor Zolin?"

"Roger that," said Uncle Timothy. "My protected sources and human assets have surveilled the Mutant Ninja Turtle and have his twenty."

"Huh?" said Tommy.

"That must be his lame code name for Zolin," suggested Storm. "Because the billionaire is teenage."

"And *twenty* is CB-radio code for location," I added, which I knew because I like old movies.

"Timothy?" said Mom, sounding exasperated. "What's his address?"

He gave it to us and Mom repeated it to the taxi driver.

"It is two minutes away," said the driver. "Why you no walk?" Then he mumbled something about "lazy Americans."

"Meet us there," Mom told Uncle T.

"Why?" he asked, totally dropping his secret spy gibberish.

"We have reason to suspect Viktor Zolin is the art thief who grabbed the four masterpieces out of the Hermitage Museum."

There was a pretty long pause.

"Understood," said Uncle Timothy. "I will meet you on the sidewalk in front of his building."

We drove maybe six blocks.

"Here we go," said the cabbie.

Mom gave him a huge tip because the ride had been so short.

Then the five of us tumbled out of our cab in front of a super-swanky apartment building. It was ten stories tall and in the heart of a ritzy, high-rent district known as the Golden Triangle on the banks of the Neva River, not far from the Hermitage Museum.

"This is the most expensive real estate in all of Saint Petersburg," said Storm, who has been known to memorize apartment listings on the web in her spare time.

Uncle Timothy was waiting for us on the sidewalk with his six friends, three of whom were still wearing those ridiculous rubber Putin masks. Maybe Tommy was right. Maybe the guys had really, *really* bad zits.

"How'd you get here so quick?" I asked.

"I'm a pro, Bickford. A pro."

"Do you know which apartment is Zolin's?" asked Mom.

Uncle Timothy nodded. "Yep. All of them!"

CHAPTER 59

"Zolin will meet us upstairs in the penthouse," said Uncle Timothy.

Mom arched an eyebrow. "Does he know we're coming?"

"Affirmative. I thought it best to let him know. We don't want him siccing those wolfhounds on us, so I called ahead."

"I don't think that was our best play, Timothy."

"Relax, Sue. Calm down."

Mom's ears turned pink. She hates it when somebody tells her to calm down. (Yep. Storm inherited most of her stormy temperament from Mom.)

"Besides," said Uncle Timothy, gesturing toward his six colleagues, "we have backup. Zolin's just a kid. My men are all very heavily armed."

When Uncle Timothy said that, his six henchmen tapped their chests, bellies, butts, and shins—all the places they were concealing clinking weaponry.

All we Kidds had brought with us were our quick wits, our keen minds, and our martial arts expertise. Luckily, Uncle Timothy and his army of musclemen were on our side.

We stepped over some wolfhound poop in the lobby and rode a gold-plated elevator up to the tenth floor.

The elevator doors opened directly into a lavish penthouse suite. Viktor Zolin, the teenage oil billionaire, was waiting for us in a giant living room where the ceiling looked like the topping on a lemon meringue pie.

And, of course, he was weeping.

"That horrible weeping clown painting you hung in the Hermitage," said Beck. "Is that supposed to be a self-portrait?"

"I d-d-don't know w-w-what you're talking about," Zolin blubbered. Then he blew his nose in a very frilly pillow.

"Cut the waterworks," I said in my best tough-guy voice. "We know what you did."

"W-w-what? What did I do?"

"You stole the four missing masterpieces from the Hermitage collection," said Mom. "Then you pretended to be so upset about the missing paintings, you had us thrown in jail. You named my husband as the prime suspect. And you did all of that because you knew that the Kidd family always finds whatever treasure we're hunting— no matter where that hunt leads or how long it takes."

"Chya," said Tommy. "We're good, bro."

"Admit it," said Mom. "You were surprised to learn that Professor Thomas Kidd and his family were in Saint Petersburg on vacation.

You didn't want us investigating your crime so you tried to turn us into the criminals!"

Zolin sneezed into his pillow and wept some more. "But w-w-why?" he sputtered. "W-w-why would I do such a thing? I love art!"

"No, you don't," I said. "In fact, you hate it."

"That's why you hung those hideous paintings in the gallery," said Beck.

"And," I continued, "we know the reason you did all the nasty, evil, and despicable things you did. It's extremely psychological. Storm?"

She stepped forward. "Would you like to hear your complete profile?"

"It's pretty gnarly, dude," added Tommy.

"No, thank you," said Zolin, snapping his fingers. A servant hurried in with a gold-plated tissue box that was filled with silk scarves instead of Kleenex or Puffs. The young tycoon dabbed at his eyes and dried them.

"Come on," I said, eager to prove that the theory I'd cooked up after reading that travel guide was right. "Art killed your parents. So you hate art!

Bada-bing, bada-boom. Case closed."

"Do you know what else I hate?" asked Zolin, totally composed.

"That cold pizza with all the fish and little red eggs on top?" said Tommy.

"No! I hate nosy treasure hunters. You are correct, Mrs. Kidd. When I learned that you and your meddlesome family were visiting Saint Petersburg, I pulled all the strings I could to have you detained. And, trust me, when you are a billionaire oil tycoon in Russia, you have plenty of strings to pull! All the strings money can buy."

"We're going to report you to the authorities," said Mom, totally unruffled.

"Good luck with that," sneered Zolin. "Half of the government officials in Russia are on my payroll. Half of the people in this room too."

"Actually," said Uncle Timothy, "more than half. There are seven of us, only five of them."

Surprise, surprise. Uncle Timothy was still a no-good rotten traitor.

The three goons in the rubber masks finally yanked them off.

No wonder they'd been hiding their faces and not saying a word.

They were the same Zolin thugs we'd met on the icebreaker on our way up to the North Pole!

CHAPTER 60

Viktor Zolin decided it would be a shame to imprison us before we could see the rest of his elaborate home, so he took us on a tour of his fifty-something-room apartment.

We had an armed escort, of course—Uncle Timothy and those six Zolin soldiers. One of the guys from the ship kept trying to spook us.

"Accidents happen in Saint Petersburg too, Mrs. Kidd. To pipes. To people. Pipes get broken. Noses too."

"You realize, of course," said Storm, "that you

used that same basic threat on us when we were at the North Pole."

"So?"

"You need some new material, man," said Tommy. "You're like barely even *trying...*"

The thugs shoved us into room number forty-something.

I have to admit that Zolin's ten-story apartment was pretty incredible. All the toilets were basically gold thrones. There were more paintings than you'd find in most museums. Unfortunately, all of them were stacked in piles on the floor. The walls themselves were white and barren except for all the giant video screens hooked up to gaming devices.

Hey, if you were a thirteen-year-old billionaire, you'd probably have an Xbox or PlayStation in every room too.

"Wait a second," said Beck, staring at a Picasso on top of what could've been a Monet or maybe a Manet. I always get those two guys confused. "That's Picasso's *Naked Woman on the Beach!*"

"Where?" said Tommy, suddenly interested.

"That's the same stolen painting we saw in the art gallery in China!" said Storm, accessing her vast memory banks. (I wrote about that in our last book, if you haven't read it yet. What are you waiting for?)

Beck turned to Uncle Timothy. "You know, the one you sold to the cultural minister while you were pretending to be a triple agent working for him."

"And then," said Uncle T proudly, "I helped Viktor steal it from the Chinese."

I had to admit, I was sort of impressed. "Wow. You really are a quadruple agent!"

Uncle Timothy took off his mirrored sunglasses so he could blow on them, fog 'em up, and give 'em a quick polish. "What can I say, Bickford? I'm good at what I do."

"You mean selling yourself to the highest bidder?" said Mom sarcastically.

"It's what we all do, Sue. You find a sunken treasure chest, you take bids from museums. I find a spare Picasso, I auction it off. It's simple economics. Supply and demand."

"And," said Zolin, "as you have seen, with Timothy's help, I have amassed one of the largest art collections in the world. But it's not enough. I want more. *More!*"

"What do you plan to do with it?" asked Mom. "Open your own museum?"

"Don't be ridiculous. I'll leave that to those silly fools at the Hermitage. No, your nosy brats are correct. Art killed my parents. In return, I intend to kill art—all that I can get my hands on. Soon, this Picasso and Monet and the four paintings I removed from the Hermitage will be sent downstairs to the boiler room. Oil is such an expensive way to heat a house. But I have found an even more expensive fuel: oil paintings!"

"Dude," said a stunned Tommy. "You're seriously going to burn them?"

"Yes! All the paintings *and* their fancy wooden frames. They will heat the bubbling water in my fourteen hot tubs!"

"You can't do that!" I said because Beck was too busy hyperventilating in horror.

"Oh yes, I can! In fact, I must. As you know from your psychological profile, I am an extremely twisted teenager."

All of a sudden, he started bawling again.

"Because I miss my mommy and my daddy!"

Tears were sputtering out of his eyes like he was a human lawn sprinkler.

Mom wasn't buying it.

"You're faking."

Zolin suddenly smiled. "Right again, Mrs. Kidd. It's a gimmick I use. Gives me an advantage when negotiating deals." He gestured toward a large conference room where the walls were, of course, white, blank, and bare. "Speaking of deals, I would like to negotiate with you."

"For what?"

Uncle Timothy answered for Viktor Zolin (maybe he was paid to do that too): "The art Thomas found when he stumbled on the Enlightened Ones' secret treasure trove."

"How'd you know about that?" asked Tommy.

"Easy. I tapped your mother's watch and her satellite phone."

Beck shook her head in disgust. "You're a snake, Uncle Timothy."

"It's just business, Rebecca. You'll understand one day."

"She already understands that there are more

329

important things than money," Mom snapped. "Like friendship and loyalty."

"And family," said Beck.

Zing! Even Uncle Timothy couldn't come up with anything to say to that, because he knew they were right.

CHAPTER 61

"Tell me, Mrs. Kidd," said Zolin, "where exactly did your husband find the Enlightened Ones' secret cache of precious paintings?"

"We don't know," said Mom.

"And did your husband receive a cash reward for all the treasures he liberated from the Enlightened Ones?" Zolin asked.

"He will," said Mom. "The art museums the pieces were stolen from and their insurance companies will be very pleased when the artworks are safely returned to their proper homes."

"Pocket change compared to what you fools

could get by selling the paintings to us," snarled Uncle Timothy.

"I'd rather be a fool than a skeevy sleazeball!" snapped Beck, who was furious. As the artist in the family, I think she was the one who was the most horrified by Uncle Timothy and Viktor Zolin's art-destruction plans.

"Enough!" said Zolin. "You are professional treasure hunters. Money talks, everything else walks. I will double whatever the museums and their insurance companies are offering you!"

"Whoa," said Tommy. "Double?"

Zolin shrugged. "I just have to pump oil a little faster up in the Arctic Ocean. If some spills on a walrus or turns a polar bear into a brown bear, who cares? I will make money, money, money! Some of which I will give to you."

Mom nodded slowly. Thoughtfully.

I couldn't believe this. Was she actually considering creepy Viktor Zolin's oily offer? Would she let Uncle Timothy destroy everything the Kidd Family Treasure Hunters stood for? We weren't just about the money. We were about trying to make a difference in the world and returning beloved art treasures to wherever they really belonged.

"I need to contact my husband," said Mom. "Arrange a few details."

Zolin smiled. "Please do."

Mom tapped her wristwatch. We heard Dad's receiver ringing.

Mom started humming while she waited for Dad to pick up.

"Hello?" said Dad.

Mom kept humming.

He hummed something too. Then Mom picked up the humming. Then Dad took over. It was like a humming duet!

AH, MY FAVORITE TUNE!

Or something far more clever.

I glanced at Storm. She shot me a sly wink.

We both knew that Mom and Dad were communicating in some kind of secret musical code—the same one they'd used before in our adventures.

"Hey—" Uncle Timothy cut in.

But before he could continue, Mom stopped humming and said into her watch, "Honey, I think I may have found a new buyer for the stolen artworks the Enlightened Ones had in their storage space."

"But," said Dad, "the museums and their insurance companies will pay—"

"Half of what I will pay!" shouted Zolin. "Name their price and I will double it."

"Is that you, Mr. Zolin?"

"Yes! I'm a billionaire oil baron! I can buy anything and everything I want! Anything, I say!"

"Very well," said Dad.

Zolin raised his fists in triumph, then looked over at us. "And you Kidd kids agree to this as well? I do not want any of you changing your minds."

Storm spoke up. "If Dad says we're in, then we're in."

The rest of us nodded. We didn't know what Mom and Dad's plans were, but we trusted that they knew what they were doing.

"I've already crated the paintings," said Dad. "But I haven't alerted the museums."

"Good move, Thomas," said Uncle Timothy.

"Hello, Timothy. I can assume that, in my absence, you are looking out for my family?"

"Like always. I'm also looking out for you. I brokered this deal."

"Does that mean you want a share of the profits?"

"Nothing outrageous, Thomas. Twenty-five percent would be fine."

Beck groaned in disgust. It was hard to believe how slimy Uncle Timothy was, even though he'd shown us time and time again.

Dad didn't seem to mind. "Make it fifteen and we have a deal," he said.

Zolin flicked his wrist at Uncle Timothy. "I'll make up the difference."

"Deal," said Uncle Timothy.

"I'll need a little time," said Dad. "I have to call in a few favors to arrange a cargo plane. Then it's at least an eleven-hour flight from where I am to Pulkovo Airport there in Saint Petersburg…"

I could see the wheels in Storm's head turning already. Which places were an eleven-hour flight from us?

"We will wait for you," said Zolin. "And until you arrive with all of my new masterpieces, do not worry—your family will be my houseguests."

He sliced his finger across his throat, signaling Mom to end the call.

"Got to run, hon," she said. "Love you."

Zolin clapped his hands. His minions pulled out that arsenal of weapons they'd been concealing.

We weren't really going to be houseguests until Dad showed up.

We were going to be hostages.

CHAPTER 62

We spent a very long day and night in Viktor Zolin's apartment.

Even though the walls were lined with TV screens hooked up to awesome, super-high-tech gaming devices, it wasn't a fun sleepover. Video games have never really been our thing. Beck and I had spent three-quarters of our lives living on a ship. We were having too much fun going on real adventures to let avatars made out of pixels have all the fun for us.

Mom suggested that we all do our best to keep Zolin "extremely busy."

"If you guys keep bugging him," she whispered

when we had ten seconds alone in a seventh-floor bathroom (one of at least fifty in Zolin's ten-story apartment), "he won't have time to drag any major masterpieces down to the furnace before your father gets here."

"Then what's the plan?" I asked.

"When your father arrives—"

Mom couldn't finish her answer. Our armed guards found us.

"Here you are!" said one of the unmasked goons who had menaced us on the icebreaker trip north. "Viktor wants you upstairs in the game room. I think he wants to play with you some more."

We did as we were told. But we also filled Viktor's day with a lot of stupid and annoying diversionary tactics.

For instance, Beck and I did three Twin Tirades. In a row.

Storm bored Zolin with more Russian tour-guide trivia.

And Tommy broke the thumb controllers for Zolin's prototype PlayStation Six playing Batman: Arkham Knight.

Then, finally, a full twenty-four hours after Mom and Dad's phone call, Mom's wristwatch chirped.

"He's here," Mom announced.

Dad was back in Saint Petersburg.

I had a feeling things were about to get extremely interesting.

CHAPTER 63

Zolin opened a window and leaned out to survey the street below.

"I don't see a truck. Has Professor Kidd brought the artwork? If I don't see some new paintings soon, I'm going to start weeping again!"

"Relax, Vik," said Uncle Timothy, joining Zolin at the window. "Most likely he parked around back to avoid drawing too much unwanted attention. He'll use the service entrance."

"No, Timothy," said Dad, striding into the room. "As you might recall, I always prefer the front door."

"Dad!" we all cried. But Zolin's goons wouldn't let us go to him.

"What?" said Zolin. "How did you enter my apartment building without the doormen downstairs alerting me?"

Dad shrugged. "It seems they all fell asleep ten seconds after I waltzed into the lobby."

Tranquilizer darts!

Did I ever tell you guys how good Dad is with a blowgun?

"Well played, Thomas," said Uncle Timothy, who, once upon a time, was Dad's handler at the CIA. "You always were one of my best undercover operatives."

"Did you bring me my paintings?" said Zolin. "I want to add them to the four I stole from the Hermitage Museum. My oil-burning furnace needs a lot of oil paintings for fuel."

"Ah," said Dad, acting impressed, "so *you* were the mastermind behind the theft of the missing da Vinci, Caravaggio, Giorgione, and Rembrandt paintings."

"Yes! It was simple, really. Those so-called guards in the gallery? Their loyalty can be easily purchased for a few rubles. Although that one lady was tough. She demanded euros because she wanted to buy a new 3-D television set in Germany. She likes *Masha and the Bear*. But enough bragging about my criminal genius. Where are the paintings the Enlightened Ones were hoarding that you tracked down?"

Dad grinned. "Not so fast, Mr. Zolin. First,

you show me my money. Then I'll show you the paintings."

"W-w-what?" whimpered Zolin.

"It's how we always do things, Vik," explained Uncle Timothy. "Makes for a better exchange if both sides can see what they came for before they give up what they brought."

"Fine," said Zolin. "I can write you a check or wire the funds into your account."

"Thanks but no thanks," said Dad. "This is to be a cash-only transaction."

"No paper trail," said Uncle Timothy. "Smart, Thomas. Smart."

"Thank you, Timothy." Dad coolly eyed the six armed goons ringing the room. "Good afternoon, gentlemen. Nice of all six of you to join us. If you don't mind, I have been away from my family for far too long. I'd like a moment to properly greet my wife and children."

"Go ahead," said Zolin, giving us a royal flick of his wrist. "You have my permission. But hurry up. My furnace grows cold."

Dad flung open his arms at the center of the room. "Okay, guys. Group hug."

Mom quickly ushered us over to him and we all hugged it out.

And that's when Dad shouted, "Duck! Now!"

CHAPTER 64

We hit the deck.

When Dad tells us to duck, we don't ask questions!

The second we were sprawled on the floor, about three dozen Russian *politsiya* officers in SWAT team combat gear stormed into the room, their weapons already trained on Zolin's six armed guards.

Because a few seconds ago, Dad had alerted them to how many bad guys were in the room!

Uncle Timothy ran toward the open window.

Quick-thinking Mom pressed a button on her watch and a thin cable slithered out. She whipped it around his legs before he could jump through the window and escape! With a thud, Uncle T face-planted on the floor; three soldiers instantly surrounded him.

"Hands up!" shouted the woman leading the charge. "All of you!"

Okay, you're not going to believe this. The top cop? It was Larissa Bukova! That's right. Our former tutor and extremely chatty tour guide. Only now she was dressed in a police uniform and bulletproof vest.

"Viktor Zolin," said Larissa Bukova, "you are under arrest for stealing four priceless masterpieces from the Hermitage Museum."

"Ha!" laughed the teenage billionaire. "You can't prove that."

Four more cops marched into the room, carrying the four missing paintings. Beck was happy to see the officers were wearing white lint-free gloves like all good art handlers wear.

"Here is your proof, Mr. Zolin," said our ex–tour guide who was really an undercover cop. "Plus, we have your verbal confession here." She pulled a digital recorder out of her bulletproof vest. "You are going to prison for a long, long time. But let us look on the bright side. By the time you are released, you will be old enough to drive. Actually, come to think of it, when you finally leave jail, you will be old enough to live in a home for senior citizens. Take him away!"

"N-n-no," the billionaire blubbered. "How much do I have to pay to make all of you forget about this?"

"There are some things that can't be bought, Viktor," said Mom. "You'll learn in jail that money doesn't always talk."

Zolin quickly turned off the waterworks and looked defiant. He stomped his foot on the floor. "I didn't do anything wrong."

"Yes, Viktor," said Major Bukova, "you did."

"But what about my doggies?"

Inspector Gorky strolled into the room wearing

his rumpled raincoat, even though it was sunny outside. "We'll take good care of your wolfhounds," he said. "But we will no longer allow them to poop on the floor in our art museum!"

Zolin wept. For real this time.

Now Gage Szymanowicz, the Russian civil defense minister, joined the crowd crammed into Zolin's upstairs game room.

"We thank you, Kidd Family Treasure Hunters, for your assistance in returning our national treasures." He marched over to Uncle Timothy. "Now we will return one of your national *disasters*."

"Look, Gage," said Uncle Timothy, "we can make a deal."

"No, we cannot. Our SVR intelligence agency has already made a deal with your CIA. You are going back to your cell in the super-maximum-security prison, with even more security on top."

"Thomas? Sue?" pleaded Uncle Timothy. "Do something! The beds at ADX Florence are made out of concrete!"

"Sure," said Mom. "At Christmas, we'll send you a concrete throw pillow."

"You know, Sue, you're no fun as a blonde."

Four officers hustled Uncle Timothy out of the room. Inspector Gorky ordered the *politsiya* officers to handcuff and remove Zolin's minions.

"Thank you, Kidds," said Gorky. "I apologize for ever placing you on my suspect list."

"In a fist, all fingers are equal," said Storm. Don't ask me what that means. I think it might've been another Russian proverb.

"You were just doing your job," said Mom.

Gorky nodded and left with his troops. Minister Szymanowicz and the four cops in white gloves took the paintings back to the Hermitage Museum.

Finally it was just us Kidds and Major Larissa Bukova left in the room.

"So, you were like an undercover cop the whole time?" said Tommy.

"*Da*. I work for Minister Szymanowicz, as does Inspector Gorky. At first, we all thought you six Kidds were greedy American art thieves. That you journeyed to Russia only so you could pillage and plunder our priceless treasures. But as I came to know you, I realized that not all

354

Americans are bad. In fact, you six are very, very good."

"Major Bukova and I have been working together on this sting ever since Mom called yesterday," said Dad.

"For the safe return of our treasured artworks," said Major Bukova, "I and the people of Russia will be forever grateful."

One by one, she gave us each a big bear hug.

Tommy was the last in line.

She gave *him* a kiss—on the cheek.

EPILOGUE

CHAPTER 65

Since Dad missed our first trip to the North Pole, we chartered a boat that had a helicopter and went back.

We did our own Kidd family walk around the world.

Then we ate a fun family dinner of raw fish and blubber mixed with mac 'n' cheese. It tasted pretty much like how it sounds.

After dinner, Dad *finally* told us where he'd found the Enlightened Ones' secret treasure trove.

But I'm leaving that part out.

Because now it's your turn.

Do you know where Dad found all that stolen art?

It's not any place I would've guessed. (Those Enlightened Ones are extremely clever.)

Oh, I almost forgot, Dad did give us **one more clue** that might help you on your quest. Here it is:

It has one of the world's only blimp parking spots.

(If you're really stumped, I'll stick the answer at the end of the book, on page 364. But if you have any plans to be a treasure hunter like us, you'd be hunting down the answer right now!)

By the way, when Dad found the Enlightened Ones' secret hiding place, guess what else he found besides all that art.

That's right. More clues.

Apparently, the E-1s have looted so much treasure over the years, they have hiding places all around the globe!

Which is fine by us. The Kidd Family Treasure Hunters are already planning more incredible adventures to awesome parts of the world that are waiting for us to explore them. (Hopefully, next time it won't be so cold, and the menu won't have blubber on it.)

Also, Beck wants me to say that even though our job is pretty exciting, it's about more than just finding old, expensive things. We get to see and do things that can maybe help others.

Remember all that video we shot in the Arctic? Well, we edited it all together into a documentary and gave it to environmental groups that are working to save the Arctic from climate change. People are watching footage of the awesome landscape and animals that they would normally never get to see. The documentary is being seen all over the world!

That's pretty cool.

Always remember this if you ever set out on a treasure hunt of your own: The earth is the greatest treasure of them all.

THE ANSWER!

O kay, readers, after seven clues and a million guesses, here's the location where Dad found the stolen goods stashed by the Enlightened Ones.

Ready?

Are you sure?

I don't want to spoil anything if you're still thinking of figuring it out for yourself!

Here it is...

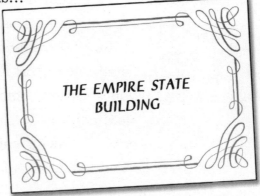

THE EMPIRE STATE BUILDING

Good work, treasure hunters!

NOTE FROM THE KIDDS

Thanks so much for reading about our latest adventure!

We figured you had a fun time working out where the secret stash of art was hidden, but we have an even **cooler** puzzle for you to solve!

Us Kidds have been spending months tracking down clues—and we just might have *finally* discovered where the Enlightened Ones' secret home base is located.

Using the code on the following page, find the letters in the book that will spell out the location of the hideout.

THAT'S DEFINITELY A TREASURE WORTH HUNTING, HUH?

THE CODE

Here is the code for finding each letter to spell out the secret location. Good luck!

1. Chapter 33, paragraph 6, sentence 1, word 6, letter 3

2. Chapter 9, paragraph 1, sentence 1, word 8, letter 4

3. Chapter 61, paragraph 6, sentence 1, word 9, letter 1

4. Chapter 22, paragraph 4, sentence 2, word 14, letter 5

5. Chapter 2, paragraph 5, sentence 2, word 28, letter 3

6. Chapter 27, paragraph 2, sentence 1, word 6, letter 4

7. Chapter 50, paragraph 4, sentence 1, word 5, letter 1

8. Chapter 13, paragraph 3, sentence 3, word 8, letter 2

9. Chapter 42, paragraph 2, sentence 4, word 8, letter 2

10. Chapter 26, paragraph 1, sentence 1, word 18, letter 4

11. Chapter 16, paragraph 5, sentence 2, word 4, letter 5

12. Chapter 59, paragraph 7, sentence 3, word 5, letter 1

13. Chapter 35, paragraph 6, sentence 2, word 1, letter 1

14. Chapter 48, paragraph 2, sentence 2, word 16, letter 8

15. Chapter 11, paragraph 4, sentence 2, word 6, letter 3

16. Chapter 57, paragraph 2, sentence 2, word 18, letter 2

17. Chapter 3, paragraph 5, sentence 2, word 10, letter 1

18. Chapter 64, paragraph 5, sentence 4, word 4, letter 1

19. Chapter 29, paragraph 3, sentence 1, word 9, letter 1

_ _ _ _ _ _   _ _ _ _ _

_ _ _ _ _ _ _ _

YOUR CLUE

I t's time to think like a Kidd! Enter our competition to come up with your own secret base that's related to museums like the ones featured in the Treasure Hunters series. There are lots of great prizes up for grabs! To enter, use your knowledge about that location to create a clue in 25 words or fewer. Here's an example:

> *Guarded by a skeleton "tyrant"*
> *nicknamed Sue,*
> *it's hidden under the tomb*
> *of the Pharaoh's son.*

GIVE UP? MY SECRET BASE IS BENEATH THE RE-CREATION OF UNIS-ANKH'S TOMB IN CHICAGO'S FIELD MUSEUM OF NATURAL HISTORY. AND I ONLY USED 16 WORDS!

To enter THE TREASURE HUNTERS SECRET HIDEOUT COMPETITION, you must fill out an entry form and submit the following information by 14 October 2016 at www.jamespatterson.co.uk/treasurehunters:

• the correct response to the Enlightened Ones' secret home base, using the code on pages 366–367 (remember, your decoded answer is not case-sensitive, but spelling counts!);

AND

• your own clue and answer describing a museum-related location that contains enough detail to be accurately solved, just like Storm's!

Our judges will choose the most creative and humorous entry. Visit the website to see the great prizes up for grabs!

See the Competition's Official Rules at www.jamespatterson.co.uk/treasurehunters

IF IT WEREN'T FOR ROTTEN LUCK, RAFE KHATCHADORIAN WOULDN'T HAVE ANY LUCK AT ALL!

READ ON FOR A SNEAK PEEK

ROUGH START

Welcome to THE PAST! Don't worry, we didn't go that far. Just three weeks earlier, to be exact.

I was at the tail end of a pretty lousy summer, which is *supposed* to be the best time of the year for most kids. Me, not so much. Camp Wannamorra had been a disaster, and my time at The Program in the Rocky Mountains just about killed me in six different ways. (Well, okay, just *one* way, but still…)

None of that was the worst part, though. That happened on the Friday before school started, when Mom took me to Hills Village Middle School. We had a meeting scheduled with Mrs. Stricker and Mrs. Stonecase so I could get re-enrolled there.

You remember Mrs. Stricker, right? And Mrs. Stonecase too? They're the principal and vice principal of HVMS. They're also sisters—for real. That's like getting twice the trouble for half the price. Not to mention, if there was a Worldwide Khatchadorian Haters Club, they'd be the president and vice president.

So anyway, as soon as I was stuck inside that lion's den (I mean, sitting down in Mrs. Stricker's office), I got a two-ton piece of bad news dropped on my head.

"If Rafe wishes to come back to Hills Village Middle School this fall," Mrs. Stricker said to my mom, "he'll have to be enrolled as a special needs student."

And I was like, "Say WHAT?"

But Stricker wasn't done. She kept going, like a tidal wave of meanness that just couldn't be stopped. "Whether he'll finish middle school on time or have to put in an extra semester or two— or *more*—well, we just can't say at this point," she told us.

And then I was like, "Say WHAAAAAAT???"

I don't know what they call it at your school. IEP. SPED. Special Education. Barnum & Bailey's Three-Ring Circus. At HVMS, the kids have plenty of names for it—just not ones they say when any teachers are around.

And now I was in it.

I tried to talk Stricker, Stonecase, and even Mom out of making this horrible mistake, but they wouldn't budge. Mom wasn't being mean about it or anything. I know she wants what's best for me. She just said I should give it a try.

"We'll see how things go once the school year starts," she said. "Who knows, maybe you'll even like it."

Which is such a MOM thing to say.

In the meantime, if you're thinking this story is all about bad news, don't worry. Some cool stuff happens too, like that first kiss, and some other things I haven't even told you about yet.

But so far? My school year was off to the worst start ever.

And it hadn't even started yet.